ANGER MANAGEMENT

ANGER MANAGEMENT

ADRENALINE RUSH™ BOOK THREE

LAWRENCE M. SCHOEN
BRIAN THORNE

LMBPN
DISRUPTIVE IMAGINATION®

LMBPN Publishing
PMB 196, 2540 South Maryland Pkwy
Las Vegas, NV 89109

Version 2.00, September 2022
ebook ISBN: 979-8-88541-846-1
Print ISBN: 979-8-88541-848-5

THE ANGER MANAGEMENT TEAM

Thanks to our JIT Readers

Wendy L Bonell
Diane L. Smith
Dave Hicks
Deb Mader
Jeff Goode
Peter Manis
Jan Hunnicutt
Zacc Pelter

If We've missed anyone, please let us know!

Editor
The Skyfyre Editing Team

This book is dedicated to all the scientists, doctors, nurses, and first responders putting themselves in harm's way to protect us all during this current pandemic that threatens to engulf the world.

Nobody deserves more recognition at this moment than they do.

CHAPTER ONE

"I want you to change me into a clone of Tycho!"

Coop almost dropped his cup, spewing coffee in a stunned spit take that would have done any golden-age comedian proud. He lurched upright on the upholstered blue and gray chair that had been cradling him so comfortably. After a long life working in Hollywood, he imagined he'd seen or heard every crazy idea that studio heads, wide-eyed mystics, or born-again post-modern newer-agers had ever come up with. Dr. Acorns' statement proved him wrong.

"That doesn't make any sense. First, even I know that cloning people still isn't possible, and second, even if it were possible—which it's not—Tycho's been in a coma for, I don't know, forever? Seriously, Jess, you're the one who told me she's brain-dead!"

He'd had his feet propped on a nearby end table. They plummeted to the floor as he swept his legs off the table, nearly knocking Potato over in the process. At the last moment, he scooped up the blue and green striped alien fuzzball and held it close to his chest. He got to his feet and glared at Jess, her words echoing impossibly.

"Mr. Cooper, please, just hear me out."

The two humans faced off in the most luxurious room on the entire moon, the presidential suite of the *Palais Titan*. They'd paid for it with money acquired from selling technology that had belonged to the Box, after eliminating their robotic presence from Titan. She was a world-class virologist who had been researching an alien virus to end all disease. He was a sixty-something actor who had been dying of liver failure after decades of alcohol abuse and agreed to take part in her experiment. Unseen but no less present was their point of intersection, an artificial personality that had taken up residence in Coop's head, a side effect of an alien virus she'd injected him with. The personality was named Dyrk and was the product of endless hours of action-adventure films.

«*I heard it too. Clone her into Tycho? That's what she said. Is she insane?*»

Shut up, Dyrk, Coop thought to himself and his viral echo.

"Jess, I know you've been through a lot these last few days, what with discovering a cure for, well, nearly everything. And learning that the alien robots that hired you had decided to kill you instead. And then escaping them. And then helping Dyrk and me to wipe them from Titan."

«*That pretty much summarizes it.*»

What part of "shut up" is giving you trouble?

As usual, Jess wasn't privy to the conversation going on in Coop's head. "It's a lot, I get that, but you're not making sense now."

"What doesn't make sense to you, Mr. Cooper? The virus that healed you and is making you younger, that same virus is going to kill me within a few days' time."

"No, right, I get that, but maybe Dyrk can remove the virus from you. Wouldn't that help?"

"It's too late. It's already restored my body to the peak of genetic health."

"But that should be a good thing. Peak of health. Fit as the proverbial fiddle. Hale and hearty. Full of piss and vinegar."

«Piss and vinegar?»

It's an expression. Also, shut up!

"You're missing the key distinction, Mr. Cooper. Not the peak of health. The peak of *genetic* health. Which in my case includes an incurable congenital disease that is now likewise at its peak, and as a result it will kill me in days. That only leaves the one option that I've come up with."

"But Jess, it's not possible!"

She stepped closer and took Potato from him to cradle it against her chest. The alien creature nuzzled against her neck. "No, it's just never been done before. No one has ever had this virus available to them, or Dyrk's ability to guide it, or Potato's pheromones to empower it."

Coop gestured to the unconscious young woman with ebony hair who was sprawled on a blue chaise lounge in the next room, just visible through the open doorway. "None of which has helped Tycho. She's still in a coma."

"Exactly," agreed Jess.

"Exactly what?"

«Seriously, I'm not following any of this.»

"Tycho has been in a coma since before she received the virus. Arguably, she doesn't have a mind to guide it to restore her to her genetic best. I do."

"But you said your virus is killing you."

"It is. I need Tycho's."

«But Tycho's virus only works for Tycho.»

"Dyrk says her virus only works for her."

"Exactly!" Jess folded her arms across her chest, her expression showing that she'd won the argument, though Coop didn't see how. "Which is why I want him to change me into a clone of Tycho!"

CHAPTER TWO

Alhiz'khlo'tam was one of a few thousand Clustera to have survived the destruction of their home world at the hands of the Box. He and his middle daughter, Antella'nestra, were the only Clustera on Titan. They were also the sole members of his familial pod to have lived through the massacre. Back home, his daughter had been a valued artisan. She'd been one of the world's best creators of the colandracel, the prized crystalline instrument. None but the most skilled performers could use it to give voice to Heaven itself. He, Alhiz'khlo'tam, had been among his world's most accomplished players.

Now, that was ancient history. The trauma of so much horror and death had altered them both. Antella'nestra had retreated somewhere into her mind, never speaking again. Her hands still flew across the sonic loom that was always near, but they did so like a cleverly designed clockwork automaton. She lacked the joy that had once flowed through her every movement. Whether the crystals she wove into each new colandracel still elicited the divine was unknown—Alhiz'khlo'tam had never played any of them. As tragic as his daughter's fate was, his own transformation was more amazing. Once a talented artist whose music had brought hundreds of thousands to ecstasy, he had arrived on Titan stripped of his ability to play and found work as a bouncer in a syndicate club. It had been a long climb through the ranks, filled with double-dealings and betrayals, until he had replaced the previous head of a crime syndicate that ran a third of the moon. His enemies and his associates—a crime boss of his stature did not have *friends*—knew him as Al.

In a secure room deep beneath the surface, in a location known to no other, Alhiz'khlo'tam tapped into the spaceport's own systems, running software that ceaselessly scanned for any bit of data that might suggest Box activity. Over the years, there had always been a small but steady stream of information, often tracking the comings and goings of the three Box personae that had established their research "ranch" on Titan. That had ended a day ago when Cooper, a recent human arrival, had somehow defeated them all. Al's scanners had been silent since.

Until now.

A klaxon announced a small vessel emerging from null space above Titan. Telemetry poured in, revealing a craft too small to be a passenger vessel or an automated transport. In many ways, it resembled a missile rack strapped to a null-space engine. Seconds after it had arrived, twenty "missiles" separated from it and fell toward Titan. Al's software attempted to identify the projectiles, wasting processing cycles comparing them against its database of armament before moving on to other Box hardware. Not missiles, but twenty instances of a Box avatar that had never visited this star system before, different from the three varieties of Box that had lived on Titan. The Box named this entity Doos, and among the race of machine intelligences, it acted as a judge and jury, dispensing what they perceived as justice. Thousands of Doos had arrived on Clustera once, bringing about the destruction of that world. Al never imagined he would see their like again, least of all on Titan. Now they fell from the sky. The Box had returned!

CHAPTER THREE

"Jess, maybe it would help if you start from the top."

"What do you mean?"

"I mean, break it down for me. Out loud. You're clearly stuck in your own head,"

The young researcher sighed. "Okay. Let me see…" She began to pace again as she talked.

I wonder if she even knows she does that.

"You, Mr. Cooper, have been infected by a version of the virus that has completely integrated with your central nervous system. It has become sentient, like a conscious echo, and goes by the name Dyrk. Dyrk's presence seems to be tied to certain stressors that trigger neurophysiological reactions."

Coop nodded and stroked his chin. He enjoyed it when she dumbed it down enough for him to keep up with her scientific prattle. She liked big words, lots of them in quick succession. Coop did not, and he tended to zone out. He did his best to stay focused this time.

Jess continued. "When you arrived on Titan, you presented as a sixty-something-year-old human male. You suffered from late-stage cirrhosis of the liver and all the other anticipated effects of a lifetime dealing with an alcohol use disorder. You were then injected with the virus and subsequently underwent multiple stressors that placed extreme demands upon your body. Now you present as a robust, healthy male in his late forties, early fifties, with no physical ailments. You are at the peak of health and getting better every hour."

"Yes I am. So far, so good. Keep going." Coop had refilled his coffee and took a sip. He liked helping.

"By contrast, Tycho is a comatose human female just under twenty. She has been infected with the virus for almost the same amount of time as you but with no change in her state whatsoever." The doctor gestured at the back bedroom, where the young woman lay in a vegetative state.

Coop had avoided that room as much as he could. It was weird to see someone so young and pretty look so lifeless. It made him squirm and feel all kinds of icky.

He set his cup down and put on his best concentration face while Jess continued her monologue. He steepled his fingers under his nose to project maximum attentiveness.

"Finally, there is my situation, which is perhaps the most complicated."

«Says the woman that doesn't have an alien invader living in her mind.»

Concentrate, Coop thought back. *One of us needs to understand this.*

"My illness has returned…with a vengeance. In fact, it appears that the virus has intensified and advanced my congenital disorder."

Coop nodded slowly. "I think I'm following. Go on."

"I didn't see it before, but now I can't ignore the truth. I was wrong. The virus doesn't cause the body to heal."

Cooper scoffed. "Of course it does, or have you forgotten my perfect liver and even better looks already?"

«As if she could have missed those.»

"That's just it. Your liver is perfect. It's exactly the liver that you are supposed to have. It's right there in your genetic blueprint. I now see that's how the virus works. It doesn't simply heal. It's more subtle than that. It restores things to their original design, wiping away the deviations of time and environment until you're at your body's optimal level."

"So how is that a problem?"

Jess sighed. "You're not paying attention, Mr. Cooper. My health issues aren't like yours were. I don't have a liver that I've abused with decades of alcohol and a plethora of other bad choices."

Ouch. I resemble that remark.

Jess continued. "I have a genetic disease. It's hardwired into me, part of my particular blueprint. It is as much a part of me as the color of my eyes or my fingerprints."

"But weren't you getting better, maybe for a bit?"

"I'd been treating myself with a pharmaceutical cocktail that managed to retard the progress of the disease for months. And yes, initially, when we were fleeing for our lives, because I was scared out of my mind, the virus partially activated in me. I think it read how my body was responding to the drugs I'd taken and ramped up that response for a time. Then it began looking through my genetic code and tried to put that so-called optimal version of me in place."

"So, what are you saying?"

«She's saying that the virus is functioning in her, just without the benefit of a bonus personality living in her head to help direct it.»

"I'm saying that I was better off before I injected myself with the virus. I'm saying it's working hard to ensure that my disease kills me, probably within a week."

The things Jess had been saying fell into place for Coop. The virus that had given him his life back was going to take hers away.

«Coop, slide over.»

Without waiting for agreement, Dyrk took control over Coop's body.

You could let me pretend I have a choice.

«Sorry, buddy. There's a damsel in distress. No time.» He stood. «Jess, Dyrk here. I'm confused. Why would your virus have waited for you to be scared before it activated? There's been plenty of adrenaline running around to trigger it.»

"Because I modified each version of the catalyst through the movies I showed it while it was incubating inside Potato. You are the product of action-adventure films. Tycho was shown exclusively war movies with a heavy post-apocalyptic bent. My version of the virus was shown horror films. Which, in hindsight, was not the best choice."

But if the virus is working in her, why doesn't she have an echo like you living in her head?

«You may be surprised to hear this, but Ben just asked a good question. Why hasn't your virus manifested the way I did in him?»

"I suspect your situation is unique. I believe—though it's almost impossible to prove—that the neurological-altering effects he experienced from null-space syndrome allowed for you to take up residence alongside Mr. Cooper in the same mind. In other words, he and I both have the virus, but he also acquired a parasite."

I second that description.

Dyrk ignored Coop. «Parasite?»

Jess shrugged. "Initially. Though it's clear you're moving to establish a more symbiotic relationship because of your ability to interface with the virus to effect positive changes. That's what gave me the idea of changing into a clone of Tycho."

«Because I can manipulate the virus to effect deliberate changes in the host? I suppose that might work, if I'm able to interface with your virus.»

Relief shone in her eyes. "So, you think there's a chance? I mean, it's a lot more than just altering the virus in a vial of blood."

«That's what we need to find out. Can I communicate with your virus well enough to convince it to work off the template of Tycho's DNA instead of your own?»

Jess chewed her nails for a moment. "I don't have much to lose. What do I need to do?"

«Just stand there and look pretty.»

Jessica's eyebrows climbed her forehead. They almost met in the middle.

Whoa! Danger, Will Robinson. Danger!

«Um, just stand still...please.»

"Better."

Even I knew not to say that.

Jessica complied, and Dyrk concentrated. He leaned close, his mouth and nose all but in contact with her face.

«Just breathe normally. Try to relax.»

Dyrk could…taste the difference. Okay, maybe "taste" wasn't the right word, but it was close. It felt different from Tycho's virus from when he had held a vial of her blood. This was unique to Jessica, and also different from the version that had created him and ran through Ben's body. Affecting Ben's virus had been effortless. Over the past few days since waking up, Dyrk had been able to heal his host's liver, reverse the aging process, repair broken limbs, and even alter the genetics of Ben's eyes to pass a retina scan.

What Jessica was asking was so much easier, in theory: convince her own virus to prioritize the mission of Tycho's virus instead. He tried to do it, imagined touching the virus in her with his will and making the changes so that it could instead use the blueprint of Tycho's DNA. It was like trying to mold dry clay. It didn't want to take on a new shape. It reasserted itself every time he let go of it. He kept trying, but her virus began attacking his efforts. It was as if he were an invader in her body. Dyrk stood his ground, but the earlier headway he'd made crumbled bit by bit.

It went on like that for several minutes. Jessica's legs shook and sweat gathered on her brow.

Dyrk tried harder, but her virus kept resisting. He grunted in frustration and stepped back. «I'm sorry, Jessica. I'm afraid I might be making it worse.»

CHAPTER FOUR

When Dyrk's connection to her virus snapped, Jessica swayed on her feet. Her face contorted in pain and exhaustion caused by the viral echo trying to manipulate her genetic foundations. Dyrk flinched, certain that she had experienced his efforts like he'd kicked her soul right in the stomach, after first scratching her eyes out with a rusty spoon.

She placed a hand on the sofa.

"Whoa! That is not fun. I'm going to go sit for a minute. After that, I need to check some data." Jessica's legs were unsteady as she walked to the bedroom where Tycho rested. She closed the door behind herself.

Tired from his exertions, Dyrk retreated to the cognitive peanut-gallery and Coop slid back into control. He turned and found Potato standing on the ottoman, shifting from side to side on its dozen tiny legs.

Coop picked up the furball and let it climb to his shoulder, where it perched with its furry face snuggled against his neck. It felt good. Not that he'd ever admit it.

The actor resumed his own pacing.

"There's a larger problem here, Dyrk."

«Do you mean the fact that Jess might die because I can't get her DNA to shift? Because, yeah, that seems like a problem. One I am quite aware of.»

"No. Not that problem. I mean the broader, more philosophical problem that comes from any set of bad choices."

«Philosophical? Who are you and what did you do with Ben Cooper? What do you mean?»

"I mean, saving Jessica may not be worth the cost that has to be paid."

«Ben, I'm programmed like a one-dimensional action hero. Unless our ears deceived me, you just said you want to let a young, attractive, and absolutely brilliant woman die. That makes no sense to me.»

"That's because you've never felt pain, Dyrk. Emotional pain. The kind that makes you feel like someone slowly torched pieces of your soul with one of those fancy little things pastry chefs use."

«That does sound painful.»

"What I mean is, you might be able to change her DNA, but at what cost? What if the pain and torture of going through it breaks her mentally? Is she still the Jessica we know and admire if her mind is crippled?"

«Whoa. That is deep, Ben. I think I get it. This is like the conflict in a movie. It's the source of tension that has to be overcome. Am I right?»

"You're not wrong, but this isn't a movie."

«This is that whole human experience thing you keep telling me about.»

"Dyrk, now you're getting it."

«Thanks, Ben. I mean, for teaching me. About pain. It seems to be a big deal with human beings.»

"Yeah. It is a big deal. So big that I've made a lifetime of bad decisions trying to ignore it. Maybe it's time I pay attention to it in other people."

Jessica returned. She had a tablet in her hands and a worried expression on her face.

Coop didn't like it. "Jess, what is it?"

"I got a message here. It says it's from Al."

Al was a xenon, the Titan-based crime boss that they had partnered with. He was also the guy responsible for their arrangements to get off the planet on the next ship bound for Earth.

"Well? What does it say?"

"Run."

«*Cryptic.*»

"Why would he tell us to run?"

As if in answer, the double doors to the hotel suite flew open. Something had shattered the locking mechanism from the outside.

Coop spun to face the threat. On his shoulders, Potato pranced nervously.

A Box avatar unlike any they had seen previously stood in the doorway.

Coop gulped audibly.

Behind him, Jessica did the same. "Um, I think that's why he wanted us to run."

The Box wasn't tall, nor was it overly broad. Every inch of its metallic carapace spoke of violence and aggression. It was malice incarnate. There was very little human, or even human*oid*, about it beyond a rough silhouette. A half-dozen weaponized limbs sprang from its body, maneuvering about like octopus tentacles. Instead of legs, its lower torso flowed into a base that split into a rugged set of treads, one to either side, like a tank. It was without debate an avatar built for the use of force.

"I am Doos of the Box. I have come to recover our property." The Box's voice thundered into the suite.

"What property would that be?" Coop challenged.

"I am here for Potato and for Dr. Jessica Acorns."

"Too bad. You can't have them. They're living beings, not property. Also, they don't like you."

"I have a contract," Doos replied. Its voice had become softer and less resonant.

«I hate these guys and their damn contracts.»

"Yeah? Good luck trying to take us to court. Now leave before I call the police."

Doos rolled into the hotel suite's foyer. A deep hum emanated from it, like a low and slow doppler effect. The frequency of the hum dropped, lower and lower until it either ended or fell below the threshold of Coop's ears.

A moment after the sound stopped, Coop gasped. His pulse raced as if someone had reached into his chest and clutched his heart in an iron grip. His legs felt like they'd turned to water, and he stumbled. Potato held on tightly. Coop flailed, reaching for a nearby coffee table to keep on his feet, clinging to it for dear life. He fought to catch a breath. He'd never felt so frightened.

«Ben? Are you okay? What's happening?»

Terrified, Coop thought back, but couldn't elaborate. It was like both his brain and body were shutting down, incapacitated by waves of fear. The only reason he didn't pee himself was that he'd gone just a few minutes before.

The Box edged closer and paused. It raised one of its less lethal-looking limbs, some kind of sensory device. A series of red lasers flickered, touching on everything as it scanned the room. Coop couldn't move his head, but his eyes tracked the beams. The lasers stopped when they ran across Jessica, who stood frozen to the spot.

Her shaking body did nothing to hide her own terror. Coop thought she must be paralyzed with fear, same as him. It was what kept her from jumping out a window. That and the fact that the hotel was on Titan and the suite didn't have any windows.

Doos rolled past Coop, halving the distance between it and Jess.

"Ah, Dr. Acorns. Excellent. I confess to having a dilemma. You see, even a token display of resistance would be sufficient for me to justify exterminating your consciousness permanently. Frankly, you will be much easier and more economical to transport if you are deceased, but I would prefer to extract some of your knowledge beforehand."

«Okay, Ben, I got this. There's no way we're going to let this tinker toy threaten, let alone abduct, Dr. Acorns. I'm coming through.»

Dyrk shoved Coop's consciousness aside and took charge. He tossed Potato onto the lush sofa with one hand while the other snatched Ben's saucer and coffee cup.

He hurled the dishes in the general direction of the invading robot.

Doos must have possessed a full three-hundred-and-sixty-degree sensorium. Without turning, it whipped one of its weapon tentacles around and shot Dyrk's missiles out of the air in a pair of dainty little explosions. The china collided with Doos' bolts of lethal energy and puffed out of existence.

It was fortunate for Dyrk that the entire hotel suite was covered in knick-knacks and assorted decorative detritus. His hands flew as he advanced across the room, throwing one tacky decoration after another toward his opponent in a barrage of carved owls, porcelain clowns, and ceramic hoboes. His slipper-clad feet performed a lethal tango across the marble floor, and he closed the distance between himself and the Box invader.

But Doos wasn't an amateur, nor was it a pompous alien academic like Scatola had been. Nope, it was a war machine, and its weapons obliterated Dyrk's projectiles one after another like an expert skeet-shooter.

The avatar also continued its slow march into the suite. It drew closer to Jessica by the second.

Fortunately, Dyrk had a plan.

«Jessica, get down and get out of the way,» he called to her.

Whether she heard him or not, she didn't move. She just stood there, trembling, eyes wide with blind panic. Which meant he'd have to work a little harder to save her. No problem.

Dyrk reached the suite's wet bar. His hands moved like a master in an old Kung Fu movie sending a hail of stemware and highballs toward the Box avatar.

As his supply of booze-related ammunition dwindled, Dyrk tossed a final handful of shot glasses into the air.

Doos tracked them with its mounted laser-targeting system. The glasses disappeared in puffs of dust. More of its weaponized limbs fired ion blasts and mini-lightning bolts at them with incredible efficiency.

Do not let those hit us! Coop insisted inside their shared mind. *That would be bad.*

«Ben! Hey, buddy, you're sounding better.»

Yeah. The panic began to subside as soon as you took over. I don't know what happened.

«I'm guessing some kind of infrasonics.»

Come again?

«Sound waves below the range of human hearing. They're stimulating your body's sympathetic nervous system—or they were until I took control of the body and overrode the response.»

English, please.

«Doos has some kind of fear gun.»

Dyrk had filled his arms with the last of the glassware and been hurling it throughout the conversation, inching closer to the Box with each throw. Doos disintegrated every piece until Dyrk was out of ammo.

The room quieted.

Doos lowered its weapon limbs and returned its focus to Jess.

"I hope you now understand. You cannot prevail against me. I will have what I came for."

In response, Dyrk reached behind him with one hand and grasped one of the wrought-iron barstools. In an overhand arc that pushed the boundaries of leverage, he brought it down on top of the robotic foe. The Box wobbled in place and failed to respond with a weapon-tentacle, so Dyrk struck it again and again.

Dyrk thought he'd taken out the targeting array and one of the limbs. Apparently, this Box was designed to intimidate and eliminate.

«Ben, this thing is all noise.»

It did a pretty good job of atomizing everything you threw at it.

«Pshaw, that's just some good targeting software. Which makes sense, because I'm guessing the range on its fear gun is limited. It needs to be able to get close enough to use it, but once it does, it's got no game. Tactically, I think it's a complete boob. It hasn't a clue when it comes to hand-to-hand combat.»

Dyrk raised the stool again but was forced to abort his strike. Even a boob can be dangerous when desperate. A metal spike stabbed outward from the Box's carapace, level with Coop's belly button. Fast as a viper, the spike drew blood despite Dyrk thrusting his pelvis backward.

Dyrk winced. «Sorry, Ben.»

If you keep getting my body damaged, I'm not going to let you drive anymore.

With its targeting package smashed, Doos swung its limbs around wildly. They were made of metal, and even as simple blunt instruments, they were dangerous. They weren't agile, but they would hurt if they connected. Dyrk backed up to avoid them, but the Box trundled after him. He had no intention of making a blind retreat that would back him into a corner. Instead, he leapt onto the bar.

Perched up high, Dyrk considered his options.

There weren't many, but one would be enough.

Still hanging on to the barstool, he jumped and executed a twisting somersault. He landed just beyond the blinded avatar, positioning himself between it and Dr. Acorns.

«Ha! This is almost too easy.»

Is it?

«I guess not. It is decidedly un-heroic. Huh. Should that be 'non-heroic'? Maybe 'heroic-ish'?»

Why is your grammar so terrible?

«Ben, I learned to speak from Schwarzenegger, Stallone, Chan, and Girabaldi. Why do you think I sometimes have trouble?»

Fair enough. Now, back to the main point: Hitting it now is also a great way to guarantee survival. Surviving is a very human thing to do. So, hit it!

Dyrk considered Ben's point. Then he swung his barstool. It took some time and a few glancing blows that Ben didn't deign to complain about, but Dyrk managed to beat enough of the arms into submission.

He sucked down a few deep breaths as Doos maneuvered blindly on its tracks. The Box seemed to be trying to find its way out of the suite, but Dyrk wasn't having any of it. He was Thor, armed with an enchanted barstool instead of a magic hammer. Minus the enchanted part and the amazing hair.

He let the barstool fall and used both hands to grip one of the Box's arms and rip it free. It made for a much better hammer, and Dyrk used it to club the avatar to pieces. He didn't feel noble, banging away at a blinded opponent, but he knew Coop was right and that it was necessary. He was glad no one else was there to see him do it.

At long last, Doos stopped moving. Its noises and gyrations ceased. Some internal doodad had overheated, and a portion of its carapace was hot to the touch. Wisps of smoke rose from its head.

The avatar was defeated. Its consciousness had left the building.

A calm flowed through Dyrk, and he turned to close the doors to the hotel suite in the most nonchalant way he could. One leaned a bit on its hinges. He considered fixing it, but ultimately shrugged and turned away. The suite cost enough anyway. Let the steward figure it out.

«Ben?»

Yeah, Dyrk. I'm here.

«I'm tired.»

Say no more.

Coop slid back into control of his body, and Dyrk exited stage-left.

Coop looked to make sure Jessica was safe.

She was, but she wasn't in good shape.

As her paralysis ebbed, she'd begun to move, but hadn't made it far. Jessica clung to the doorway to Tycho's bedroom. She was hunched over on her knees, and her head touched the floor. Her body shook and Coop heard her gasps from all the way across the room. He saw her wrap her arms around her abdomen.

"Jess? Are you all right?"

«I think she's been shot. Hurry, Ben!»

The actor rushed across the room and slid to a stop on the floor next to her. He gingerly put his hands on her back. "Jess! Talk to me."

Her body continued to heave and she drew in ragged breaths. "Can't…it's gonna kill me. It's gonna…kill…me!"

"No, Jess. It's not. We stopped him. He's done. Dead, or as dead as those weirdos get. You're safe now."

Jessica either didn't hear him or didn't care. She continued to be racked by sobs. She mumbled nonsensical declarations of impending doom.

«Okay, the good news is, looks like I was wrong about her being shot. She probably got hit with the Box's infrasonic fear waves right up until we killed it. That's a long time to be terrified.»

"What do I do?"

«You're asking me? Um...pick her up. Put her on the sofa. Get her off this cold floor.»

"Good idea."

Coop did as Dyrk suggested. He scooped Jess into his arms and stood and carried her to the sofa. He set her down as gently as he could amid the small army of throw pillows littering its surface.

The moment her butt hit the cushions, Potato rushed over and leapt into her lap. It nuzzled her and wriggled into her limp arms. Coop covered them with a blanket and stepped back to think.

CHAPTER FIVE

Jessica sighed and returned to the present as the furry little alien worked to get her attention.

"Potato."

"Hmmm? What'd you say?" Coop asked.

She didn't look up to find his exact location. She just lifted one trembling hand and stroked Potato's back.

With a weird clinical detachment, she murmured to herself. "Potato doesn't snuggle."

Coop hovered nearby, relieved that she was coming out of whatever panicked state she'd fallen into. "What's that, Jess?"

"Potato. It's never shown this degree of interest in anyone. Not any of the Box, and not me. Potato. Does. Not. Snuggle."

The actor looked offended. "That's not completely true. He likes me."

"Only since your virus became active. Before that, he liked you about as much as your exes. Oh my…" She dumped Potato off her lap and rushed to another of the suite's bedrooms, the one she had claimed for her temporary lab. She moved quickly, suggesting she was recovered, motivated, or both. Coop followed more slowly. He found her sprawled across the bed she'd transformed into a makeshift examination table, running a hand-scanner over her abdomen.

"Aha!

"Aha, what?" asked Coop. "What does the scanner's readout mean?"

"It means my version of the virus is more active than it's ever been. It had taken up residence near my adrenal gland, but now it's hyperactive and it has spread throughout my circulatory system."

"That's good, right?"

"Better than good," Jessica replied. "If I'm right, then Dyrk should be able to have more control in guiding the virus to remake me into a clone of Tycho."

Coop raised his hand, offering Jess a high five, but she ignored him and left him hanging. Sheepish, he lowered his hand as she stood from the bed.

"So, what happened that caused the virus to kick in?"

"Fear. Blind terror. Abject horror. My version of the virus was created after exposing Potato to thousands of hours of horror films, remember?"

"Oh yeah. I knew all that. Just like Dyrk was based on endless action flicks…I know you need adrenaline to kick things off, but you've had it before. The virus should have been working already, right?"

"Ah, but that's where I think you're wrong. Where I have been wrong. The virus isn't just looking for an influx of adrenaline like I first thought. I've tested for that in all three of us. It's a necessary but not sufficient piece of the puzzle. There's also a cognitive component that's in play. That's probably why my cinematic treatments never worked with the non-sapient lab animals. They didn't form the associations to the films that a human brain can."

Cooper nodded. Understanding dawned on him. "So, when the virus worked in me, it wasn't just because of the adrenaline. It was because of the situation I was in?"

"Exactly. A 'fight or flight' scenario releases the adrenaline, but that's only the first step. I think there is also a dynamic, situational factor. With you, with the action-adventure tropes, you needed to be in an environment of danger that also offered you something that you could fight against. I've suspected this since we fled Scatola's ranch. This new data confirms it. The virus in me is happy to work, if I'm scared out of my mind first. Textbook-style panic attack or better."

"Right. Nothing like a killer robot aiming energy weapons at you to get the blood pumping. This sounds like a terrible way to get healthy."

Jessica shuddered. "Seriously."

«Ben, I think she's right. I can sense the virus in her. It has entered a new stage. Let me in.»

Ben groaned. "Dyrk wants to talk to you. I'll be back."

Dyrk came to the fore and grabbed Jessica's hands. She raised an eyebrow.

"Do you think you can do it this time?"

«I'm not promising anything, Dr. Acorns, but it feels different. The virus is more malleable...more awake than it was before. My instinct tells me you're onto something and we need to try again. Right now.»

Jessica shrugged off the tension. "All right. Go ahead."

Dyrk leaned in, much as he had before, bringing his face close enough that he could smell her breath and ensure she had no choice but to inhale his. Communicating with the virus in her was all about sending and receiving pheromones that ordinary humans never noticed, that Ben hadn't ever produced before. He closed his eyes and furrowed his brow in concentration. He felt the virus. It was there, waiting for him. It seemed almost eager for his guidance. It had spread out across Jessica's system. It felt more...alive. More present and reachable.

He plunged in with all of his will.

Dyrk worked fast. It was much easier this time. He isolated a portion of Jessica's virus and once again introduced a sample of Tycho's virus. They seemed to get along better than the last time. Jessica's virus held off its earlier inclination to combat the foreigner. Encouraged, he nudged the virus to use Tycho's DNA as its new paradigm, and it offered no objection. So far, so good. The final step was to convince it to share the new genetic template with the other instances of the virus in her system. They all had to be on board, or there was no point beginning the larger alteration of her body.

Guiding and changing the virus was hard work. He encountered pushback as Jessica's virus again resisted the instructions from Tycho's virus, requiring him to override the resident virus. It was exhausting work. Minutes ticked by, and for a change, Ben stayed silent in their shared mind, sparing Dyrk any distraction. Dyrk kept going, exerting his considerable will. He felt the change take hold, one virus giving way to the other.

His hands shook and his knees wobbled. Minutes ticked past, but Dyrk held on.

Finally, after half an hour, Dyrk collapsed onto one knee and let go of Jessica's hands with a sigh that spoke of incredible fatigue, but also of satisfaction.

He retreated to the welcoming confines at the rear of Ben's consciousness and left the actor alone with Jessica.

CHAPTER SIX

The doctor locked her gaze with Coop's. "Did it work?" she asked.

"How should I know?"

"Well, ask Dyrk!"

"I can't. He's gone."

"What do you mean, he's gone? Where could he go? He lives inside your brain!"

"I mean, he's gone to ground. He's spent. Wiped out. Don't worry, though. He's done this before, and he'll be back once he recovers." Coop stood again and waved at the monitors she had scattered around the room. "Can't you tell if it's working? You know, with all your science…stuff."

Jess smacked her forehead and tapped on her tablet.

"Huh. Something is happening…I think it's a race."

"A race?"

"Between the virus that's doing the original work and the virus that Dyrk set to modifying that version. The initial burst of activity coincides with my panic, but the effectiveness is receding in parallel to my parasympathetic nervous system calming mc down."

"So...you need to be scared again before the instructions Dyrk gave your virus will kick in fully?"

"Not just scared," replied Jess. "Terrified."

«I don't think that will be a problem, » put in Dyrk.

"Welcome back, buddy."

"Dyrk? Is he there? Can he do anything more?"

«Tell her I'm back, barely. I feel like I went ten rounds with an entire Olympic Sumo team! Let her know that I've done all I can. Now it's up to her own virus, but I think she's right.»

"So, I just need to come up with something to frighten her?"

«Or we could wait around and the Box will come for her again, with more guns and threats of imminent death,» offered Dyrk helpfully.

Coop nodded to the unseen voice in his head. "Yeah, you're right."

"What?" asked Jessica. "What is he right about?"

"The Box. They're pretty relentless. If we don't scare you deliberately, they'll show up and do it again for real."

Jessica crossed her arms. "There are problems with both of those ideas."

«Problems?»

"How do you mean?"

"If you're creating something to scare me, and I know it's coming, will that knowledge modulate the level of panic to something below whatever threshold the virus needs?"

"I don't think that's going to matter. Dyrk thinks Doos had some kind of fear gun."

"Oh. Huh. That leaves the second problem. Repeated terror of this magnitude is going to produce deleterious side effects beyond anything the virus is able to handle in time."

Coop sighed. "In English, Jess. Please."

She tapped the face of her tablet and showed it to him. He stared at it without comprehension for a few ticks and added, "*Spoken* English."

Jessica explained, "My cortisol levels are through the roof. They're already coming back down. Once the virus is fully activated, it will restore any physical damage like loss of bone density, but the psychological damage could be permanent."

«What kind of psychological damage?»

"What kind of psychological damage?"

"Flashbulb memories. Intense, full-body memories of the event that are more vivid than everyday stuff. It's more like re-experiencing the trauma than remembering it. Extreme PTSD kind of stuff."

"I've known people like that," agreed Coop, more serious than Jess had ever seen him. "It can be its own kind of living hell. So, let's take that off the table. It's not worth it."

«What if it's a choice between that and her syndrome killing her?»

As if echoing Dyrk's thought that she couldn't hear, Jessica responded, "That may not be something I have a choice over."

Coop had no answers and needed to think. He turned on his heel and stepped back into the main suite, where he knelt beside the remains of Doos. It had ceased to smoke, and things had cooled off enough that he didn't mind getting close.

He examined the extensions that littered the floor.

Five of the six arms had interchangeable, plug-and-play attachments that represented an arsenal of alien technology. Some fired semi-standard projectiles. They had mechanics similar enough to conventional weapons that even he could identify them. They exuded death.

A pair looked like they shot something other than bullets. He recognized them as the rapid-firing energy weapons the Box had used to shoot his bar glasses. "Fancy stuff. This is gonna fetch a pretty penny. It should make Al happy."

Then he looked at the sixth and final extension. It didn't look dangerous. In fact, it looked like some kind of scanner. It was mounted on an extendable and flexible arm with a release button. Coop pushed it, and the device fell into the palm of his hand.

He stood and waved it around the room. Nothing happened.

"What the hell is that thing?"

Jess walked in with Potato cradled snuggly in her arms. The little alien seemed like it was trying to bathe her with its tongue. It was both adorable and icky.

The scanner emitted a pinging noise that almost caused Coop to drop it.

"Whoa."

As Jess got closer, the pinging grew louder. A display screen was lit on the back of the device. It showed a smear of color that seemed to track her path toward Coop.

He pointed it away from her and the colors faded. When he pointed it back in her direction, they reappeared.

The doctor took the device and studied it, walking around the room and noting changes on the screen. "Okay, that answers the question of how this Doos found us."

"It does?"

"This is a gene-sniffer. If I had to guess, I'd say it's calibrated to my DNA. Potato's too, by the look of it. It led the Box right to us."

"How did it do that?"

Jess took a breath and looked like she was about to launch into a detailed explanation, complete with the verbal equivalent of a dozen or more illuminating slides. Then she must have considered her audience and settled on a simple answer that, in all likelihood, would still go above his head.

"It compares a template of me to tiny bits of DNA that living creatures leave behind in the air when we breathe. Patterns of concentration and dispersal allow it to construct a genetic vapor trail that shows where the target's been and how long ago, and leads to where it is. Think of it as the most sophisticated bloodhound you can imagine."

"It can track Potato too?"

"Even easier with Potato. Its template is the primary one the sniffer is using. There's nothing like Potato's DNA anywhere else on Titan, whereas tracking me would require a higher degree of discrimination to dampen the number of false positives from other human DNA."

Inside Coop's head, Dyrk chimed in. *«Which means they'll find us again. The one thing the Box know better than anyone else is what makes Potato tick.»*

"Dyrk says they'll keep coming."

"He's right," agreed Jessica. "Assuming there are more instances of Doos on Titan, it has no reason to stop. Nothing matters more to the Box than Potato and what it represents. Now they can smell where we've been."

"So, we're back to one of your adrenaline rush situations," replied Cooper. "Fight or flight. Do we stay here, build our defenses, and attempt to take out whatever they send at us, or do we make a run for it and get you and Potato back to safety?"

"I'm their secondary goal. You heard Doos. They'll settle for my body. It's Potato that they want. We knew that going in. The Box will stop at nothing to get him back. They'll just keep throwing more and more resources at us until we're overwhelmed, even if it means the death of everyone around us. They'd consider that justifiable collateral damage. Remember, they see this as the equivalent of a holy war."

«It's against my nature to run from conflict,» explained Dyrk. *«But she's right. In this situation, I think our only option is to mount a...tactical redeployment.»*

Coop smirked. "You mean run away."

«Your words. Not mine.»

The actor shook his head. "He won't say it outright, but Dyrk agrees with you. Flight, not fight. So...you and Potato, can't we just bundle you both into an environmental suit and slip off to a new spot?"

Jessica considered. "Not unless the new spot is hermetically sealed."

«Like a spaceship.»

"We've still got several days before the next shuttle to Earth is loading," Coop pointed out.

"What?"

"Oh, sorry, Jess. I'm just shooting holes in Dyrk's idea that we hide out in a spaceship."

"Huh. Actually, that could work."

"Hello? Still several..."

"No, of course, obviously... That doesn't mean we couldn't buy a little time by hiding out in a different shuttle until then."

«See? It works. We just rent a cabin. It makes sense in a place like this. Real estate and construction on Titan are expensive. We'll rent a room on a shuttle that's grounded for repairs or some such thing but would like to still generate some income. I bet they sell the space for ultra-private meetings and clandestine rendezvous all the time. It's kind of sordid, but that might work to our advantage. Besides, I find sordid things fascinating.»

"I don't know..."

"What don't you know?" Jessica asked. The frustration of hearing only one side of Cooper's internal dialogue was evident from the pinched look on her face.

"Dyrk thinks we might be able to find a room that rents by the hour."

Jessica groaned. "Why does he always propose hiding out in brothels?"

"I don't dwell on it much. Besides, you raised him."

CHAPTER SEVEN

Jessica retreated to her lab to research the availability of rental spaces on grounded shuttles. This left Coop and Dyrk alone to think. Whether they liked it or not.

«Ben, I think we need a Plan B.»

"Our primary plan is your plan. Why, all of a sudden, do you think we need a backup? This does not inspire confidence. Is something wrong with your plan?"

«Of course not. It's a great plan. Still, you know the old saying. 'The best laid schemes o' mice an' men gang aft agley.'»

"Gang of what?"

«It means 'shit happens,' Ben.»

"Why didn't you just say that? Okay, so, a backup plan…" He began pacing the length of the room. "You know…"

«What?»

"If Plan A is to isolate Jess and Potato so that DNA sniffer can't find them, what if Plan B makes it certain that they get found?"

«That would be a stupid, stupid plan. What, are you thinking we can ambush them one after another? We don't even know how many avatars Doos brought with it. I was able to beat one of them because it

was all strategy and no tactics. I don't know that I'll be so lucky if it shows up in force. The last thing we want is for a dozen killer Box to find Dr. Acorns and Potato.»

"Not if it finds them everywhere."

«If I had control of our body, I'd choke us right now, and we would deserve it.»

Coop patted the air with his hands. "Dammit, give me a minute to explain. I don't mean we let the Box find either of them. I mean we make sure they find their DNA all over the damn place. Everywhere. It's in hair, right? What if we shave Potato and leave its fur all over the freaking spaceport? It should have the Box running around in circles chasing his DNA."

«Ben, you are less stupid than I thought, and I live inside your brain, so take that for what it's worth.»

"I have no idea how to take that. So, I choose to take it as a compliment."

«You do that. Now call Jessica in here so we can tell her the plan. We need to move on this.»

"Right. Hey, Jess!"

The doctor appeared in the doorway, a small note card in her outstretched hand. "I've found several potential shuttle cabins that would serve our needs."

"That's great, but that's only part of the plan."

"I don't understand."

"Dyrk and I have come up with an auxiliary plan. Well, I guess it's more of a supplemental plan."

"A supplemental plan?"

"Exactly."

"Does it involve a bar fight?"

"No."

"Does it involve a brothel or naked women of any variety?"

«She gets us.»

"No, but I like where your head's at."

Jess sighed. "Okay, I'm listening."

"We let the Box find your DNA. And Potato's."

Jess massaged the bridge of her nose. "And now I'm sorry I listened."

Coop threw up his hands. "Will anyone let me finish explaining my plan?"

«Maybe you need to work on your delivery. You do tend to bury the lede.»

Jess waved for him to continue, but the motion lacked enthusiasm.

"As I was saying. We let them find your DNA by taking samples of your hair and Potato's fur and leaving them all over the spaceport. We send them off chasing ghosts while we secure you in a sealed environment."

Jess tapped her finger against her lips for a few seconds. Her face took on a pained expression. "This is a good idea, Mr. Cooper, in principle."

"I know! So, why do you look like it hurt you to say that?"

"It's complicated. There are different kinds of DNA, and it depends on which kind the sniffers are sniffing for."

«What's she talking about?»

"Dyrk doesn't understand what you mean."

«Oh, and like you do?»

"Strands of human hair don't have DNA, not what we normally mean when we talk about DNA. It doesn't have nuclear DNA, just mitochondrial DNA."

"Nuclear, like a bomb?"

"No, Mr. Cooper, as in inside the cell's nucleus."

"Oh. So, my plan won't work?"

"It might, if the Box sniffer is checking for both nuclear and mitochondrial DNA. If only the former, my hair won't distract it. Your plan still works with respect to Potato, though. Its hair strands do have nuclear DNA."

"Why does Potato's fur work that way?"

Jess shrugged. "Potato's an immortal alien, remember? That's the least of the differences between its biology and ours."

"So you're saying my plan might or *might* work for you but that it *will* work for Potato?"

"Exactly. All we have to do is create enough false positives to make sure we keep them busy for as long as possible. Let me get Potato."

Jessica returned a moment later with Potato, a large bath towel, and a set of battery-powered hair trimmers she'd found in a vanity of one of the suite's bathrooms.

Potato no longer looked happy. In fact, it looked as if it sensed imminent doom.

"I think it knows what's about to happen," Coop observed. "Poor guy. Better its hair than mine. Sorry Potato, it's time to take one for the team, buddy."

Potato did not look relieved by this sentiment.

«I'm not sure nobility and sacrifice are part of its makeup,»

Jessica draped the towel over the ottoman and placed the furry alien atop it. She worked gently but efficiently, and Potato's green and blue zebra-striped fur came off in large, soft clumps. The shearing revealed Potato's bare flesh for all the world to see.

"It's...purple," Coop noted in wonder.

Jessica sat back and examined her work. "It's more like lavender."

"Isn't that purple?"

"It is a shade of purple, but you're a guy. So, yes. Lavender is purple."

She returned to trimming the depressed-looking xenon. "Oh, damn! Sorry, Potato." Jess jerked her hand away.

Coop looked over and saw a small nick in Potato's purple flesh.

Jessica picked up Potato and examined its underside. The little alien had a dozen retractable feet that squirmed in the air, desperate to avoid being shaved like the rest of it. "Those are adorable. Weird, but adorable. Now let me check that laceration."

Jess set Potato down and looked at its back where she'd cut it a moment before.

She grunted in surprise.

"What?" inquired Coop.

"The cut's...gone, not even a mark to show where it'd been. Potato's already healing."

Coop looked on in awe. "Wow, that's even faster than I healed when you cut me back in your lab."

Jess nodded and set Potato back down. She applied the trimmer to the nape of her neck, cutting the tresses that flowed down her back like fire and letting them fall amid Potato's blue and green fur. She set the trimmer aside and mixed and bundled the pile of hair in both hands. "Hand me something to stuff this into. There's more than enough here to cover the entire spaceport. Considering how advanced most Box biotech is, I'm guessing the sniffer is so sensitive that you shouldn't need more than a single strand to attract it." She paused as Coop ran into one of the bedrooms and returned a moment later with an open pillowcase. "How do you plan to distribute the hair?"

"Dyrk knows the blueprints to this entire place, including the primary air circulation unit and its backups. He and I will check out the shuttle options you've researched so we pick the best place to stash you and Potato, and all the while, we'll be saturating the spaceport with your hair and Potato's fur. Once we've emptied the pillowcase, we'll swing back here to take you both to your temporary new accommodations. Hopefully, the Box will be too busy chasing their tails to notice us when we make the move."

«Don't forget Tycho,» added Dyrk.

"Right, and Tycho too."

A knock came at the door.

CHAPTER EIGHT

Everyone froze and stared at the suite's entrance.

«Sadly, none of us have x-ray vision,» noted Dyrk.

Coop silently agreed and remembered that Doos had broken the lock.

The handle began to turn, and the door swung inward on its damaged hinges. Coop let Dyrk take over his body, and the viral echo reached for another barstool and raised it high.

It wasn't a Box letting itself into the presidential suite of the *Palais Titan*. It was Al, the alien crime boss who'd arranged for them to be there.

The xenon entered, all seven feet of him, dressed in black slacks and a black sequined shirt that outshone everything but his glossy shoes. If he hadn't been so tall and projecting an aura of casual and effortless danger, Coop might have cracked a joke. Instead, everyone let loose with a massive sigh of relief.

"Hi, Al," Coop remarked, retaking control and sending Dyrk into the background.

The onyx-skinned Clusteran waved a hand in greeting. He looked at the *debris au* Doos that littered the floor. "Cooper," he replied. "Dr. Acorns." He stepped around the carnage, careful to protect the shine on his shoes.

"As I feared, one of the new Box arrived here too. I take it you were unable to heed my advice?"

Jessica frowned. "You mean 'run'? We appreciate the warning, but there wasn't time to act on it."

"My apologies, Dr. Acorns. This extension moved more swiftly than I'd anticipated." He gestured at the main body of the defeated Box. "This is Doos. It's a representative of the Box legal system. The closest parallel in your world would be...a combination bounty hunter and privateer. It is fully empowered to do whatever it chooses in pursuit of its targets."

"That would seem to include using projectile and energy weapons that are banned on Titan," observed Jess.

Al's expression turned stony. "Doos has no regard for collateral damage or potential litigation. If it happens to blow out an exterior wall of the spaceport to get what it wants and kills dozens of innocents in the process, so be it."

«That's just dandy.»

"It has a well-deserved reputation for being unstoppable even when outnumbered hundreds to one."

Coop shook his head. "That seems like a bit of an exaggeration. I took out this one by myself."

«Ahem,» murmured Dyrk in their shared mind.

"I assure you, it is not," responded Al. "I speak from firsthand experience. Two hundred instantiations of Doos arrived on my home world and all but wiped out a population of four million Clustera."

"Holy crap!"

"Indeed. There are twenty of it on Titan," continued Al. "Seven were aimlessly wandering the main avenues of the spaceport while the other thirteen extensions have taken up positions at each of the spaceport's main exit gates. They are harassing anyone and anything that attempts to come in or out."

"Sniffers!" exclaimed Jess.

"Excuse me?"

Coop jumped in. "Al, this Doosfus had a DNA sniffer that we think can detect both Jess and Potato. That's how it found us. Jess thinks it must have tracked their genetic scents."

Al looked annoyed. "So, not wandering aimlessly at all." He glanced again at the remains of the defeated Box. "That explains how it was able to get to your hotel so quickly. It must have, quite literally, caught your scent. Damn. This complicates things."

"Wait, there's something I don't understand," Jess broke in. "If there are more of it, why didn't this extension notify the others once it had found us?"

"Ah, that has a simple explanation, Dr. Acorns. Part of the reason I chose the *Palais Titan* for you is because it's shielded."

«*Shielded?*» inquired Dyrk.

"Shielded?" repeated Coop.

"Precisely. From the moment Doos rolled into the lobby, it was cut off from its other extensions. There was never any danger of it summoning reinforcements. I came here with the intention of slipping you out of one of the hotel's lesser-known access points and taking you to an underground bunker. I have a safe house buried in the Titan terrain beyond the surface's warehouse district, less than a kilometer away. From there, I could sneak you onto an Earth-bound shuttle in two days. If Doos can track your spoor, though, I don't see us being able to get out of the spaceport."

"So your plan's a bust," stated Coop. "Not to worry, we've got a plan of our own. Two plans. A main plan for hiding and an auxiliary plan for confounding the sniffers."

A faint trill sounded, and Al raised a hand for silence. He pulled out his personal data device, tapping at the screen almost as quickly as Jess worked on her own tablet. He frowned. "Evading their DNA sensors may not be enough. Doos has flagged the tickets I acquired for your travel and will be informed should you attempt to use them. Worse still, my sources indicate that it is offering bribes throughout the port to anyone who can provide any information about your whereabouts. Substantial bribes."

"I can't stay here much longer," remarked Jess. "Its sniffer found us once, and it will do so again. Mr. Cooper, I think we need to go ahead with your plan and hope we don't run into someone who realizes who we are and turns us in for the reward,"

Al shook his head. "Even if nobody recognizes you and you're able to hide, Doos just has to wait you out and grab you when you activate your tickets."

«Did I mention things were dandy? They just keep getting dandier.»

The alien stepped further into the room and scratched his head.

"All right. Let me see what I can do. I have certain…resources. It might be possible to find you alternate passage. Though, if you're not seen boarding that shuttle at its departure time, the Box will work out that you're still here and redouble its efforts to find you."

"No problem," assured Cooper. "We just have to be sure Doos sees us boarding as planned, albeit at the last minute, right when they're closing the doors. Can you create a diversion, so its extensions are too busy to stop the shuttle from taking off?"

"I could, but that won't work, Cooper. Even if you boarded the shuttle and it departed this moon, one or more Doos would commandeer the next shuttle and follow."

"Exactly. Except, it won't matter because we won't be on the shuttle."

"But you just said—"

Coop cut the Clusteran off with a single word. "Decoys."

Al's response was as deep-throated a laugh as Coop had ever heard.

"You get it, right? So, all we need to do, in addition to hiding

Jess and Potato and messing up the sniffers, is find people to use our tickets and take our place. Then while Doos flies off after them, we'll have all sorts of other options open to us. Only thing is, I don't know how to recruit our decoys. It's pretty dangerous."

"That shouldn't be a problem," Al assured him. "I don't imagine any difficulty finding three people willing to pose as you for a free trip to Earth, regardless of the risk."

"Why is that?" asked Jess.

Al's smile was cold. "You must remember that Titan is, at its core, a corporate entity. There's a wide divide between the two groups of humans living on this moon. Those who have profitable businesses and positions of influence or power, and others who are just scraping by, having come here under false impressions that hard work alone would yield prosperity. Most of the latter would jump at the chance to return to Earth. Sadly, few of them can afford the fare. Today, their misfortunes may be just what we need."

«Ben, are you thinking what I'm thinking?»

Coop grinned. "I hadn't thought of it that way, but now that you mention it, I think I know where we can find some volunteers."

"Excellent," agreed the crime boss. "Then I suggest we all make haste and pursue our respective plans." He handed a small comm device to each of them. "This is a direct line to me. Do not hesitate to reach out at the slightest need or if any new information comes your way. Likewise, I will keep you informed of any developments."

"You're able to track all the Doos extensions?" asked Jess.

"I am, by electronic surveillance if they are outside the spaceport and by a network of security personnel and informants within. Hmmm." He paused and nudged the toe of one shiny shoe against several of the pieces of the defeated Doos that littered the suite's foyer.

"I'll have somebody come pick these up. As before, I will pay you handsomely for them. Reverse-engineering these weapon designs could prove useful indeed."

Jessica opened her mouth to respond, but Coop beat her to it. "Sounds good. Just add it to our bank account. You've got the number."

Coop took the pillowcase from Jess and accompanied Al to the door. The way he figured it, you could never have too much money, and the last thing he wanted was Jess voicing some kind of silly objection about gun smuggling or other pesky issues of morality. Besides, he needed to distribute her hair and Potato's fur and lock down a shuttle room for her and Potato to hide in. Tycho too.

"Oh, wait a sec." Coop detoured back inside to his bedroom to pick up one of the stun batons he'd used earlier in the week on the other Box avatars.

«Smart. You never know when that could come in handy.»

Coop hurried back to the doorway and paused to wave back to Jess, holding the pillowcase and grinning. "Don't worry. We've got this."

Despite the damage it had sustained from Doos' attack, the door closed on his second attempt, albeit without a working lock. Coop turned as a faint ding indicated the elevator's arrival. He expected to find Al there, stepping into the car, perhaps holding the door open for Coop, but the crime boss was nowhere in sight.

"Weird. You think he took the stairs?"

«Never mind that. We need to stay focused on the matter at hand. You know, when it comes to that shuttle cabin, we're going to be better off picking a sleazy place than any of the nice ones from Dr. Acorn's list. Doos knows we're here in the fanciest hotel suite on all of Titan.»

"So, you're thinking it won't think to look for us in a grounded ship that rents out rooms by the hour rather than a working ship that's just down for a few days? You make a good point, Dyrk."

CHAPTER NINE

The elevator chimed, the door opened, and with his pillowcase in hand, Coop strode across the lobby.

A concierge came around his desk and ran to intercept the actor before he could leave the hotel. "Excuse me, Mr. Cooper? Please, sir, a moment!"

«Whatever this guy wants, we don't have time for it. Promise him an autograph later, and let's keep moving. We're on the clock, Ben.»

Coop hesitated just a moment, which was all the time the concierge needed.

"Thank you, sir. This came in for you. I'd have had it delivered to your room, but your check-in preferences indicate that your suite is not to be disturbed under any circumstances, and we pride ourselves on honoring all of our guests' needs." He held out an envelope marked with the logo of an Earth-based messaging company.

"I don't understand. No one on Earth knows I'm here at this hotel."

"As you say, sir. The message came in to the spaceport, tagged only with your name. It's been floating around the system for two days. As time allows, I check the guest list against any unclaimed messages. Upon discovering this one, I pulled it in and set it aside to pass along when next I saw you."

The concierge beamed at him, still proffering the envelope. He looked half like a doting puppy and half like a man who performed his duties to levels beyond the norm because, more often than not, he knew he'd reap the reward of a massive tip.

«Okay, so that explains how the message got to the hotel, but who knows you're on Titan?»

Coop accepted the envelope, trading it for his pillowcase, which the concierge accepted with the solemnity of someone receiving Holy Communion. Inside was a single sheet of paper. It was from his agent.

From: Sylvia Glaxton
To: Benjamin Cooper

What the hell were you thinking signing that contract? Aliens? Medical experiments? Are you insane? I know things have been rough, but since when are you a damn guinea pig?

I looked into that producer who has promised you a starring role in his movie. He's got no history in the business. Nothing. Nada. The production company named in the contract exists only as a mail drop. Moreover, none of my attempts to reach your new producer friend have gone through. Trust me, trying to put calls through to Titan is not cheap! As your agent, I'm here to tell you you've been suckered.

Want more proof? You should know that the promised "signing bonus" never happened. The bank transfer specified in the contract turned out to be bullshit. They stiffed you.

Bottom line, your so-called contract is null and void. Get your-

self back to Earth. If not for your sake, then mine. I'm making fifteen percent of nothing while you waste time caught up in some alien scam. You're better than that, Benjamin, or you were.

—Sylvia

"Son. Of. A Bitch!"

The concierge barely blinked. "Sir? Is everything all right?"

«What? You can't be pissed off about the money? You've socked away much more from selling Box parts to Al. You had to know there wasn't going to be a movie once you wiped Scatola off Titan.»

"That's not the point," insisted Coop. "He played me. He preyed on me. That bastard took advantage of my emotional and physical desperation."

"I'm sorry, sir?" This time the concierge did blink.

«Yeah, maybe, but you ended up on top. Healed. Younger. Stronger. Plus, together, we kicked that sorry xenon's ass!»

Coop crumpled the message and shoved it at the concierge, snatching back the pillowcase at the same time.

"You're right. I know that. It's just…there's no way Sylvia is ever going to let me forget this."

«Let's worry about that after we get back to Earth. First, we've got to outsmart this Doos jerk.»

Without another word and without a tip for the concierge, Coop continued across the hotel lobby and out into the spaceport.

CHAPTER TEN

After exiting ahead of Cooper, Alhiz'khlo'tam strode along the short hallway that accommodated the four suites on this floor of the hotel. He slapped at the elevator's call button without breaking stride and continued to the wall at the end of the hall. A quick press of his hand here and over there on the featureless wall caused a panel to recess and gave him access to the passageway used by staff for room service and other needs. He stepped inside and closed the panel before Cooper had stepped into the hall, his thoughts elsewhere.

They should all be dead.

Which would not have been optimal, but if the Box had sent Doos, Al's expectations that these humans could be useful to his larger plans had to be abandoned. No one on Titan knew the futility of going against Doos better than he did. Except... Cooper had bested Doos. More, he had utterly disabled the Box. The same Box that had ended Clusteran civilization, slain almost all his family, stripped him of his art, and destroyed the person he had been.

Cooper had singlehandedly defeated the Doos that had come to his suite.

Such a thing was unimaginable. Impossible. He'd rushed to the hotel, thinking perhaps the Doos might be satisfied retaking the creature and abducting Dr. Acorns, that he might find common cause with Cooper as a survivor.

But more than survive, the human had prevailed against a Box that had killed twenty thousand with a single extension.

How had the human managed it? What was Cooper's secret, and was it possible the human could be of even greater value to Al's goals?

He took the staff elevator into a subbasement, ignoring the shocked looks from employees who knew both that he didn't belong and that they would be wise to keep out of his way. He entered a maintenance closet and, after closing the door, he pushed aside a few items on a dusty shelf to allow a disguised retinal scanner to read his gaze. A portion of the floor slid open to reveal an access stairwell that led to a hidden subway known only to Al, Titan's other two crime lords, and a handful of their respective top-level aides.

A car had arrived by the time he'd descended, summoned by the same scan that had admitted him. Its interior lights were the sole illumination in the dark tunnel. This was by design. Those who belonged there knew the distance from the stairwell to the edge of the platform and would not be hampered by darkness. Any unwary trespassers who might stumble upon this place deserved their fate if they rushed forward and fell onto the track, meeting an arriving car as the last act of their lives.

The faint light of the car illuminated the brick of the surrounding wall, revealing that it had been painted, but it fell short of revealing its color. As he often did, Al wondered about the color, but his curiosity had never been great enough to cause him to shine a light along the wall. He boarded the car and entered his destination code, and the door closed. He was whisked through the dark. Minutes later, the car halted at a random point between existing stops, where Al pried the door open against the car's wishes and jumped to the service ledge that ran the length of the track. The door snapped shut behind him, and the car began to roll away, picking up speed. A moment more, and it was gone.

Pressing himself flat against the brick wall, Al reached high above his head, feeling in the dark for a faint change in the depth of the mortar that a human wouldn't be able to reach. He'd assumed that Big Tony and the Diamond Queen—the two human leaders of Titan's other crime syndicates—had similar, secret access points when the three of them had built the subway, one of the few joint ventures they had pursued. If they had, it made sense that he would not attempt to locate them, and his security devices assured him neither of them had ever stopped a subway car near this spot. It was another example of the healthy, mutual respect that kept things in balance.

His fingers danced, pressing places among the bricks, triggering the entrance to the lair where he kept his most precious treasure. Seeing the defeated Doos extension had filled his mind with memories of the slaughter from his home world, images of death and destruction, of discovering the mangled remains of his familial pod. The adults, knowing they were doomed, had piled themselves upon the children, hoping they might be spared. The mad, desperate ploy had failed. The weapons Doos employed had taken them all, or nearly all. At the bottom of the mound of kin corpses, he had discovered his daughter, Antella'nestra, had lived, but her mind had shattered.

Once in his sanctum, Al's destination was his daughter's room. He found her as he always did, seated at her worktable, her fingers listlessly moving in the complexities required to spin the crystal instruments that she was driven to pursue in her madness. He kissed her head, but she gave no sign of noticing. He checked the supplies of food and drink that lay nearby and inspected the closet of simple clothing beyond that. At some point in the past day, she had eaten and changed into a fresh outfit. She had tended to her ablutions and slept too. Her body knew to do these things in service to her need to continue her work.

"Antella'nestra, my dearest, something unbelievable occurred today. A human, a man who calls himself Cooper, he defeated Doos."

As with his fatherly kiss, she gave no response.

"If such an impossibility can happen, who can say what else might be possible?"

Sighing, he turned from her and moved deeper into the complex he'd built. He settled in to his workroom and the desk where he could tap into the spaceport's security systems and review the sorted results of his network of operatives. Of the now nineteen Doos extensions on Titan, thirteen remained at their positions at the spaceport's main exit gates. The other six were in motion, spread throughout the spaceport's main avenues as well as its underground streets and tunnels. Doubtless, they were making use of the DNA sniffers Dr. Acorns had mentioned, a methodology soon to be spoiled by Cooper and his pillowcase of false positives.

Except...as he watched the data, it became clear that two Doos, the two closest to the *Palais Titan,* had adjusted their vectors and would converge on the hotel. Al did not believe in coincidence. The Box would get there and ascend to the presidential suite in pursuit of their mission. This time, Cooper would not be on hand to stop them.

CHAPTER ELEVEN

Jessica found herself alone with Potato.

Relieved by the solitude, the doctor returned to her work. She still had a lot of research to do and needed to gather as much data as possible before she was forced to tear down her makeshift laboratory for the move. It would be a lot easier without the odd couple of Mr. Cooper and Dyrk hanging around.

She began by taking new blood samples from herself and Tycho. The job was made more difficult by Potato, who insisted on scrambling around and rubbing against her legs like a homicidal house cat. It kept winding around her, demanding attention while she tried to work.

"Aw geez, Potato. Give it a rest."

If it understood, Potato was not inclined to honor her request. It increased its frantic neediness. In the end, Jess had to pick it up and force the creature onto a portion of the bed's lush duvet, shaking a finger and admonishing it until it pulled its legs in and drew its tongue back inside its lipless mouth, leaving behind a lavender lump. Jessica returned to her work.

Potato's contrition was short-lived, though. It lingered there only a moment before extruding several of its legs and scrambling over to Tycho's comatose body to position itself in the crook of her arm. It settled down, more or less, opting to prop its front legs on the young woman's upper body. From there, Potato seemed content to snuggle in and track the doctor's every movement as she ran a new series of scans on the sleeping girl.

Jessica worked quickly. She didn't have time to study the data in depth, but the brief glimpses she saw told her something important was going on. It kept her mind occupied while her hands dealt with the mundane work of positioning equipment and pushing buttons.

It was that mixture of concentration and distraction that made her miss the sound of the suite's door opening. In fact, she was so engrossed with her patient that she didn't notice the pair of Doos even when they had rolled through the suite's foyer and entered the palatial bedroom behind her. Not until a pair of voices spoke in unison behind her.

"Dr. Jessica Acorns, do not move or we will be forced to eliminate you."

Jessica froze.

She did not flee. She did not fight. Terror gripped her and held her with her back to the door and the Doos extensions. The only parts of her that moved were her trembling lips and shaking legs. Some portion of her brain acknowledged that, once again, the Box must be projecting infrasonics, what Dyrk had deduced to be a "fear gun." With scientific detachment, she appreciated what a powerful weapon it was. Then all pretense of rational thought departed, and she succumbed completely.

I'm going to die. I wish Mr. Cooper was here. Oh, Lord. Please don't let that be my last thought.

"Turn around, Dr. Acorns. Slowly. Please keep your hands where I can see them."

Jessica complied. Her body pivoted of its own accord, desperate to keep the Doos avatars happy and nonviolent. Her eyes locked on the floor, seeing two sets of the same heavy treads the previous extension had possessed, treads that she could glimpse through the bedroom door where the tilted and dead machine body of the first Doos still lay.

Her knees began to shake while her heart raced. It was hard to breathe. Her chest was tight. Too tight. Air wouldn't come. Her legs wouldn't hold her upright.

I have to leave. I have to sit down. I can't be here...

Anxiety assaulted her, stripping away her ability to remain upright, and she collapsed atop jellified legs on the bedroom's plush carpeting. She still hadn't managed to look up. Her hands went to the floor and she struggled to get a full breath. The air wouldn't come.

Her vision blurred and her ears began to emit a strange buzzing noise. She commanded her arms and legs to push herself up so she might stand, might flee, but they ignored her.

Not good. This is not good. I'm going to die. Oh god, I'm going to die.

With a groan, Jessica's arms also gave out, and her torso slid to the floor. Her heart began to pound faster. Then the pain struck.

Her abdomen seized, and she writhed and moaned. Spasms racked Jessica's body. Her legs kicked of their own accord and shooting pain in the back of her eyes made her hands move and grasp her face. Her fingernails dug in, tearing her flesh. She screamed.

Her head rocked back and forth, and the Doos watched, frozen by the unpredicted display. The utilitarian-length strands that remained of her red hair fell out. They littered the floor around her as her body convulsed.

She'd never imagined such pain. As a physician, she'd asked suffering patients to describe their pain on a one to ten scale. Somehow, a tiny, detached piece of her intellect was tracking her experience, deciding the agony rippling through her now was a twenty-seven! Her body burned like it was on fire from the inside, like she'd been dropped into a volcano and swallowed molten lava. Those similes didn't explain why her arms and legs were somehow shortening. She could see it. Skin and bone and muscle were changing size and shape. Was that the source of her pain? Each finger and toe altered itself before her eyes, mutating.

The virus! she realized. *It must be doing this.*

Nearby, the pair of Doos pivoted their sensors to look at each other. Their weapons remained trained on Jessica, but they were at a loss. If their avatars had been equipped to shrug in confusion, they would have done so.

"What should we do?"

"Seize and secure Potato and deal with the human after."

"Very well."

Potato had watched all this with interest from its perch in the warm confines of Tycho's armpit. It waited patiently, shifting back and forth on its tiny feet while its long tongue tasted the air, snake-like. The Doos approached from either side of the bed with their multiple limbs extended, creating a rapidly closing net.

The avatars accelerated and closed in.

Potato jumped from its cozy abode and leapt from the bed to the floor. The Doos almost crashed into each other over Tycho's prostate form, and tangled three of their wavering limbs.

Potato's beady eyes watched the avatars attempt to unknot themselves. They wrestled and tugged, each acting as an individual before the futility of their actions registered and they attempted to solve the problem together. They freed themselves, and Potato darted under the bed.

One Doos rolled and stuck a sensor-equipped arm beneath the bed frame. All it got was a view of Potato's tiny legs scrambling over it. The shaved purple alien dashed out from its hiding place and ran between the avatar's tread assembly.

The Box attempted to seize Potato. While its limbs were equipped to deal lethal damage, less consideration had been given to manual dexterity. Potato dodged its clumsy attempts and the avatar's weapons gouged bits of carpet and flooring where Potato had just been.

The other Doos rolled around the bed to assist. It fired a stun blast from one of its weapons, and the bolt of energy missed Potato by a hair.

The first Doos smacked one of its weapons against the Box that had fired on their pseudo-deity. "What are you doing?"

"Trying to capture it."

"If you hurt it, we will be shunned, perhaps exiled."

"It was a stun blast!"

"I don't care. How are we out of accord on this? Do we want to wind up like Scatola?"

"Of course not. Scatola has been relegated to the lowest of activities."

"Exactly. Which is why I tell you this. Do. Not. Shoot. Potato! Now, come on."

They turned and found Potato bouncing on top of Dr. Acorns. The unconscious woman's body still spasmed, but it didn't deter the tiny alien.

A pair of Box sensors pinged loudly.

"This is unprecedented. There is nothing in the archive to suggest anything like this kind of behavior. All past reports indicate that Potato's routine mode is sedentary. Why is it behaving like this?"

"I do not know. Could it be related to the humans shearing its fur?"

"Possibly. That may be a distal explanation. My sensors suggest it is exuding pheromones at unprecedented rates."

"Mine as well. This is strange and beyond the parameters of our purpose. We must retrieve it and return home, so those better suited to the task may study it. We must accomplish this before the human authorities arrive and complicate our mission."

"Agreed."

The Box advanced, and Potato scrambled again. The pursuit

continued for several moments, but the avatars found it difficult to chase down the elusive alien, not least because the writhing form of Dr. Acorns kept getting in their way.

Frustrated, one of the Doos opted to loop a tentacle-like limb around one of Jessica's legs and dragged her into a far corner of the bedroom to keep her out of the way and improve their ability to maneuver.

While that was happening, Potato took advantage of having only a single pursuer and clawed its way up the duvet and back on top of the bed to return to the nook of Tycho's armpit.

The other Doos advanced and leaned over Tycho, extending its limbs in a wide arc, hemming Potato in. The creature cowered, attempting to burrow behind Tycho's head on her pillow.

It nuzzled into her skin and frantically kicked its little legs as it sought refuge under her neck.

Tycho opened her eyes.

CHAPTER TWELVE

Tycho's pupils widened, and her eyes darted left, right, up, and down, taking in the details of the situation.

Her arms came up, and she placed both hands against the chest of the Box looming over her. She bent her knees and positioned her feet against its lower torso. Her muscles uncoiled like powerful pistons. She pushed and shoved the surprised avatar away from her.

Tycho sat up.

The Doos were stunned. Their sensor readings when they had first swept the bedroom had identified this human as being in a profound state of coma. Brain activity had been at maintenance levels. Muscle tone had shown significant atrophy.

Both Box stopped moving. Their systems tried to account for a human they knew had just been comatose. Their ratiocination floundered in crisis as she rose from her bed. It did not compute. The Box hated it when things failed to adhere to calculated and logically arranged plans.

Not that Tycho cared a whit about the Box or their expectations. She didn't care about anything. She planted a hand on the mattress and vaulted off the bed in her hospital gown. Her bare feet landed in front of an avatar at the same time that her cold eyes locked on it. Upon looking into those eyes, any human being would have recognized that a decision had been made the instant they'd opened—a decision that nothing short of the hand of God could alter.

Without wasting a breath, Tycho flew back into motion. Before the nearer Doos could react, she grabbed its closest weapon, tugged it under her arm, and rotated her own body to lock it in. She hit the release button on the limb and, with a twist, popped the weapon off and pulled it to herself.

Tycho continued her spin, whirling away from the Box.

The Doos struggled to pursue. It attempted to reassess and process this new data of the impossibly no-longer-comatose woman and her efficient and predatory movements.

Tycho came to a halt, having opened a bit of distance between herself and the Box. She flicked her wrist and reversed the weapon in her lithe hands.

Without any trace of emotion on her face, she aimed at the Doos she'd taken it from and fired.

A discharge of molten metal wrapped in electricity shot from the weapon, seared its way through the Box's body, and continued through the wall into the bathroom beyond. A ring of smoke drifted from the hole in the wall and small flames licked at its edges.

The Doos examined the hole in its carapace. The placement of the damage was limited to secondary systems. It was surprised to find itself still operational, but it had no intention of wasting the opportunity. It turned the remainder of its weaponized limbs toward Tycho.

The first to fire emitted a pulse of kinetic energy that slammed into Tycho's abdomen and threw the young woman across the room like a rag doll. She smashed into a floor-to-ceiling mirror, shattering it with her impact.

Her body and the shards of glass fell to the floor in a heap.

Blood streamed from Tycho's back. It trickled along her arms where small bits of glass glittered in her skin.

Scant seconds ticked by, and those same fragments of mirror began to fall to the floor as Tycho's flesh healed and pushed them out. A heartbeat later, she raised her deadpan eyes to the Doos that had shot her.

The Doos oriented its sensors on her but paused its attack, attempting to make sense of her miraculous recovery.

Tycho didn't think about it. She didn't stand—she just straightened up and leveled her weapon. She fired again and again, her finger exerting even pressure against the trigger.

When she lowered her weapon, the hesitant Doos had been reduced to a smoldering slag of metal and ceramic.

The entire exchange, from Tycho's first blast to her destruction of the Box avatar, had taken under ten seconds. The other Doos had assessed it was not needed to put down the human and had continued its pursuit of Potato until the barrage that eliminated its counterpart. Now it stared at Tycho, its cognitions moving her in some internal Venn diagram of sets of combatants and noncombatants on Titan. It whipped one of its limb weapons around its body and began firing in a wild attempt to drive her before it, force her to seek cover, and control the woman's movements until it could trap her.

Tycho dove across the floor, dodging the weapons fire, seeking refuge in the doorway to the bathroom. She landed on her shoulder and rolled back to her feet like an acrobat.

She wasted no effort—every move was efficient and effective—and sprinted to her left across the length of the bathroom. Bullets tore the walls and floors in her wake. Plaster, dust, and shards of expensive imported tile filled the air.

Tycho slid across the marble on her knees and used the momentum to pivot back toward Doos. Its treads carried it to the bathroom door in pursuit. She aimed and struck back with her own weapon, not intending to take down the Box—because, at some level, she'd already learned a single shot couldn't manage that—but instead to engulf the end of the Box's weapon, rendering it useless as it melted in front of her cold eyes.

The Doos disconnected the useless limb and let it fall away. It switched to its next mode of attack, and Tycho was forced to leap to her feet when a jet of flame rushed out in front of her.

She backpedaled and jumped on top of the toilet tank, once again at the end of the opulent bathroom.

The added elevation allowed her to leap over the Doos' next flame attack. She landed in front of the Box in a dive and roll, pressing herself flat against the floor and sliding between its treads to emerge behind it, back into the bedroom.

Potato stood waiting for her, scampering from side to side in a state of high excitement, its tongue lolling happily.

The avatar cursed and reversed direction. It had a shot at Tycho but held its fire for fear of endangering the semi-divine alien cavorting behind her.

Tycho ignored Potato. She spun, came up on one knee, and fired at the Box. She took out its flame thrower in the first round, and the next round caught the Doos in its central carapace, driving it back. The avatar attempted to orient a different weapon on its opponent, but Tycho didn't give it the time.

While it was bringing yet another of its weapon limbs to bear, she sighted along the length of her improvised rifle and put two more bursts of searing energy and white-hot metal into the main body of the Box. Its lights went out, figuratively and literally, and the avatar rolled backward into the bathroom and bumped into the wall.

A moment later, all its remaining limbs fell limp to the floor with a crash.

Tycho never uttered a single word—she wasn't even breathing hard. She stood, walked over to the Box, and disconnected all of its serviceable weapons. She rigged a pair of slings and harnesses from torn bedsheets to drape herself with her new arsenal. Along the way, she cut her feet again and again on the mirror shards littering the floor near the bed. She did not seem to notice and did not slow.

Fully equipped, she paused to gather a frolicking Potato under one arm and stalked away. She paused long enough to gaze at the unconscious and still convulsing body of Dr. Acorns. The spasms had slowed. Silky black had replaced her red hair, and her body had shrunk to become a twin of Tycho's. The original took no interest and didn't say a word. She nudged Jessica with the business end of a weapon, and when that elicited no reaction, she exited the bedroom. Her bloody feet left dainty prints on the carpet. By the time she reached the exit to the outer hall, the wounds on her feet had healed as if they had never been. Potato licked her arm.

CHAPTER THIRTEEN

Coop looked over his shoulders every few seconds. Al had insisted most of the Box were at the spaceport's exits, with a few roaming its streets. Jess had said their sniffers were focused on tracking her and Potato. Depending on how porous his pillowcase was, he might be able to walk right past one without it caring.

«Ben, it's a cloth sack. Granted, it's got a high thread count, but it's porous.»

"Right, so...let's just not run into Doos until we're done with our errands." With visions of writhing weapon tentacles dancing in his head, Coop picked up his pace. He made good time as he wove through the crowded corridors amid the hustle and bustle of the port's more industrious neighborhoods.

He knew his destination. After all, he'd already destroyed the place twice in the past week. Standing outside the entrance to the bar where he'd caused so much excitement, Coop felt a little wistful.

"You know, Dyrk, I agree with our plan, but I kinda feel bad walking in here."

«Why? After that epic fight with the Box and all the booze and boobies you paid for, these people love you.»

"We wrecked the place. Twice. In the harsh light of sobriety, they may not be quite as welcoming as you think."

«We need some volunteers, and this place is full of humans who are down on their luck, even by Titan's standards. So, unless you have a better idea...»

Coop grunted his agreement and pushed open the door. The place was different at midday. No dancers gyrated on the stages. The music that played was soft, almost soothing, compared to the blaring cacophony it had been during his previous visits. A handful of customers sat around, more concerned with their greasy lunches than their beers—except for one guy who still looked passed out in the corner, same as he'd been during Coop's previous visits.

"I'm going to assume he just never leaves," Coop muttered as he passed the sleeping regular.

The other thing that remained consistent was the adorable bartender, Lilly. She occupied her usual position behind the counter.

As Coop strode into the room, Lilly turned to see who had entered. She crossed her arms, and her welcoming smile took on a much more suspicious expression.

"See what I mean?"

«Maybe she didn't sleep well. You don't know that she doesn't like you. I mean, what are the odds? Women love action heroes.»

"Dyrk, I have lots of experience making women angry. You'll just need to trust me on this one."

Coop held his hands up in a placating gesture and approached the bar.

Lilly didn't look mollified. "Well, well. If it isn't the human tornado. Will you be behaving yourself today, or should I just go ahead and set the place on fire to save us time?"

"Nothing like that, I promise."

She sneered at him. "What's with the pillowcase? You don't strike me like the slumber party type."

«You know Coop, you may be right. I don't think she likes you.»

She doesn't like us. *It's my face, but you started all those damn fights.*

«I know that. You know that. The thing is, she doesn't know that. Hence, she hates you. *Good luck.»*

Coop sighed and turned his attention to Lilly. It wasn't hard. She was hot.

"Lilly, I get that I have caused you a lot of trouble recently. I promise I'm here for peaceful reasons today. No fights. No broken furniture. No cops. I'm here hoping to help someone."

Lilly didn't uncross her arms, but she looked curious. "Who are you trying to help?"

«*Whom,*» Dyrk offered helpfully. Coop ignored the unsolicited grammatical advice, not least because he wasn't sure it was right.

"I'm not sure yet. I have an opportunity for someone, but I don't know many people on Titan. You do. That's why I came here. To see if you could help me find the right people."

He heard her tapping her foot behind the bar. Whether that was a good sign or bad, he had no idea.

"Go on."

"You may not believe me, but I need to find people who are looking to leave here. Three people. A man and two women who want to get off Titan and go back to Earth, all expenses paid."

The young bartender wiped a glass with a rag and shook her head. "You're right. I don't believe you."

Coop had spent his entire adult life as an actor. He could do sincerity, and in this instance, he truly meant what he was saying. He plastered his face with the most earnest expression in his extensive repertoire and leaned in against the bar. "Lilly, I'm serious. I need help, and if I can find the right people, I can help them. This isn't an opportunity for just anybody. They have to be fed up with this place and need a way out. I don't think it will be dangerous, but I won't lie. It isn't without risk."

Lilly laughed. "You really are new. That description—being fed up with life here?—could fit just about everybody who walks into this bar. Everyone comes to Titan thinking they're going to make a good living, maybe even get rich. Almost nobody does."

"Why not? The other nights when I was here, it seemed like business was booming."

Lilly looked bitter. "It just doesn't work like that here."

Coop managed to look concerned and project empathy. Winning over a bartender wasn't all that different from winning over audiences. "There's something behind that statement. What's your story?"

Lilly replied with a scowl. "There sure is, but it's none of your damn business."

«Is this how you charm women?»

Coop ignored the viral echo in his brain.

"Lilly, I know I've caused a lot of headaches for you. You don't know me. Not really. I'm a good guy. Most of the time. I fix my mistakes. Didn't I make things right here? Didn't I pay for the damage I caused, and then some?"

"Sure." She did not seem impressed by the reminder of his restitution. She grabbed another glass, wiping at it furiously.

Coop valiantly continued. "If I can help, I want to, but if you won't even take the chance of talking to me, there isn't much I can do."

Lilly's hands did not relax, but she set aside her glass and rag, and crossed her arms so tightly she jammed her hands all the way into her armpits. Consternation racked her features.

Coop nudged. "You have to trust somebody, sometime."

Lilly sighed. "You need a man and two women?"

"Correct."

"Does it matter how old they are or what they look like?"

Coop considered, and remembered how effective Al seemed to be. "No. It doesn't."

The bartender took a deep breath. "I came here three years ago with my younger brother and sister. We…needed to get out of where we were, and Titan was the first place we had the chance to go."

"What happened?"

"What happened?" she snorted. "Life happened. Our dad was an absentee jerk who spent more time in prison than with us. Then our mom got cancer. She'd had a job working with toxic herbicides for one of the big agra-combines." Lilly shook her head. "It doesn't matter. I was twenty-one and had two teenagers to take care of. My brother had already gotten in trouble with the cops a couple of times because he was a dumbass who hung out with a bunch of losers who turned out to be even bigger dumbasses. Those loser friends were paying way too much attention to my fifteen-year-old sister. So, it was time to get out."

"And Titan beckoned."

"Yeah. In hindsight, I shoulda known the deal was too good to be true."

"Was it?"

"Mostly, yeah, but not totally. My brother learned a trade and he grew up some. If you fuck up on the job on Titan, somebody dies. So, he learned quick. It turns out my sister is a pretty damn good linguist. She picks up languages like it's cool and has been working at one of the hotels as a translator. But it's Titan, you know? So, the pay sucks and the benefits are non-existent. That means we're stuck."

"And you became a pretty damn good bartender."

Lilly shrugged. "Yep."

"Where I come from, good bartenders that look like you can make a good living."

"Oh yeah? That's great, but I'm here. Not there."

"Lilly, maybe we can fix that. Give me a minute."

Coop stepped from the bar and pulled out the comm device Al had provided him. The alien fixer answered almost immediately.

"Cooper, how may I help you?" Al's voice spoke in a smooth tone through the implant in the actor's middle ear.

"I think I found our stand-ins. Am I correct that they just need to be adult humans of the matching gender?"

"Yes. It would be better if there was a passing resemblance, but my people can work with most anything."

"Okay, let me close the deal, and I'll send you a message with the details."

"Very well, but hurry. Time matters, Mr. Cooper." Al ended the call, and Coop returned his attention to Lilly, who was once again cleaning shot glasses.

He leaned against the bar again. "Okay, Lilly. Here's the deal. As you may have noticed, my friends and I ran afoul of some aliens. The Box. They're all jerks."

"The ones that chased you here?"

"Exactly. We need them to think we left Titan. We have the tickets. We have the money. What we need are people to act as decoys."

"Won't the Box be angry at being tricked? I would be, and I'd want to take out that anger on your decoys."

"Maybe. Like I said, there's some risk. From what I've seen, the Box are complete pragmatists. I don't think they'd waste resources or time on decoys, so I don't believe they'd do anything to you. Really, they're pissed at me and my friends."

"I guess that makes sense. Everything I've heard about the Box says they're cold fish.

"Exactly. Your documents will be legit. Sure, I expect the Box to be pissed off that they got duped. They're too smart to blow their whole operation by venting at you, though. If they went after random humans, they'd be kicked out of the solar system and wouldn't be able to find what they're after."

"And what are they after?"

"Me. And my friends."

Lilly tapped a finger against her chin. "And you're covering all expenses? No shuttle attendant is going to demand any extra fees?"

"The full ride. Transportation costs, unlimited onboard food and drink. I'll even throw in some cash, so you have a little walking around money when you get to Earth. Do we have a deal?"

"Okay. Let's do it. I'll need to call my brother and sister, get them packing. They won't have much, just a single bag each."

"That's fine. When they're ready, have them come to the bar. The…gentleman handling the arrangements will have somebody meet you here to get things rolling."

Coop turned to leave, but Lilly stopped him. "If this works, I owe you."

He turned back and smiled. His expression was genuine this time. He wasn't trying to convince her of anything now. "Lilly, my debts to the universe run pretty deep. You don't owe me anything compared to what I owe back. Good luck, honey. I hope you and your siblings all make something of the chance."

Coop strode from the bar. He had work to do, and for the first time he could remember, it wasn't an act.

It felt pretty damn good.

CHAPTER FOURTEEN

Al reversed his earlier route with alacrity, slapping at the subway call button of his doubly secret entrance and leaping into the car the moment it arrived. The crime boss's subway would take as long as it would take, and nothing he could do would change that.

He was certain Doos would reach the presidential suite of the *Palais Titan* well ahead of him. Whatever trick or skill set Cooper had used to destroy one of the Box's avatars earlier, Al did not believe it would suffice to handle two of them. Moreover, the question was moot: Cooper wasn't at the hotel. According to his plan, he should be distributing confounding DNA throughout the spaceport. It was a clever idea but already doomed to failure. Once in possession of Potato and Dr. Acorns, Doos would be free to ignore any false positives. It might be curious, but as a race, the Box focused on efficiency and pragmatism. With the prize already won, Doos would not succumb to distractions.

His comm trilled, and he spent a few minutes responding to Cooper, who had already lined up the decoys. He considered telling the human not to bother, that Doos had likely already abducted Dr. Acorns. Except...that didn't track. If Al believed there was no hope, why was he rushing back to the hotel? He finished with Cooper's question and disconnected, impatient to arrive.

As he neared his destination, he overrode the door control and had it open before the car had come to a stop. He hurried to the hidden door and beyond it along the route that took him to the maintenance closet in the hotel's subbasement. The handful of employees he passed on his way to the staff elevator again were wise enough to melt out of his way. He fumed and chose the hotel's top floor, using a code to lock out anyone else who might call the elevator at an intervening floor.

Why did I put them on the top floor?

He was running the instant the elevator opened, running down the hall, running through the still-damaged door of the suite, running until his eye caught the trail of bloody footprints along the floor that showed that someone, a human with smallish feet, had left under her own power, striding with a determined but otherwise normal gait. More exactly, not the gait of a struggling victim or the slow trudge of a defeated captive. Someone had escaped the pair of Box.

Al frowned. Part of his success as a crime lord on Titan owed to his natural ability to notice and recall extraneous details. In this case, he recalled the size of Dr. Acorns' shoes and compared them to the bloody footprints. It was not definitive, but the prints looked too small to belong to the virologist. Which meant that whoever had walked out was irrelevant.

The rest of the room looked no different than he'd last seen it, complete with the remains of the Doos extension that Cooper had disabled. The bloody trail originated in one of the adjacent bedrooms, and he entered it with caution in case, despite all odds, one or both of the Box was still there.

They were, and they weren't. The destroyed remains of two Doos extensions occupied the bedroom, but judging by the holes that had been blasted through one body and the melted lump of the other, neither had survived. To be sure, Doos still existed, but it had lost another two bodies. Seventeen remained. Al didn't understand why the Box had allocated twenty extensions to its mission when one should have been more than sufficient, or two, just to have backup. And yet, that was proving not to be the case. Both Cooper and Dr. Acorns had been more than a match for the same Box that had wiped out most of Al's race and seized his planet.

Except...if she'd defeated the pair of Box that had come for her—as appeared to be the case—where was Dr. Acorns?

He approached the remains of the less damaged Doos, allowing his fingers to touch mangled and melted weapon limbs and trace the stumps of otherwise undamaged arms. He acknowledged a fact that he'd noticed before but hadn't properly processed: Doos' weapons were modular. Its limbs could be configured in myriad ways with whatever armament it desired for a given task. Adding new limbs would have been easy. Removing them would likewise be effortless, which explained the stumps.

Someone took this Box's weapons.

Al turned from the dead avatar, noting the hole in the wall leading into the bathroom. He poked his head in there and regarded the additional damage, and upon exiting, he noted the shattered mirror and blood on the opposite wall. It was then he saw a small, huddled form in the corner of the room. Warily, he stepped closer. Human. Female. Black hair. Clothing somewhat oversized. He recognized Dr. Acorn's lab coat, but the human was not Dr. Acorns, though a pile of the virologist's hair surrounded her head. Whoever she was, she was breathing. Al picked up the unconscious body and carried her back through the foyer and into a bedroom that Dr. Acorns had presumably used as her lab. He placed her on the examination table and lightly tapped the woman's face. It did not rouse her.

He had a fair amount of experience with unconscious humans

—an occupational necessity in his line of work—but he had not come prepared with any of the more effective, albeit invasive, methods of inducing wakefulness, even assuming there were no other injuries.

Al recalled Cooper's second traveling companion, a teenage girl who had arrived on a stretcher. That one had appeared comatose. Was this that girl? It made a certain sense, but why was she wearing Dr. Acorns' clothing?

That was the least of the mysteries he had to solve, far behind who had left the bloody footprints. Of greater importance was determining what had become of Dr. Acorns and Potato.

One thing at a time.

Al stepped back into the foyer and picked up the phone to call the hotel operator.

"This is Alhiz'khlo'tam. Yes, you heard me correctly. I am calling from the presidential suite. I believe one of the room's residents has been attacked. Send the hotel's physician here immediately. Do it now."

He could do nothing more here. He had to leave, but he couldn't until the doctor arrived. Frowning, with the phone still in his hand, he accessed an outside line and tapped in a quick sequence of digits. The line picked up after a single ring.

"Doug? Yes, it's me. I need you to come to the *Palais Titan*. The presidential suite. Bring a van. When you arrive, recruit a handful of staff to aid you. This is a salvage operation. Three extensively damaged Box avatars. Remove them to Warehouse #3 and perform a full autopsy and dis-assemblage of each. Alert me when you're through. There will likely be medical personnel here. Ignore them and discourage them from distracting you and your team. Yes, come now."

Setting the phone aside, Al returned to the other bedroom to stand by the unconscious girl. She appeared to be sleeping peacefully. Perhaps she had slept through the arrival of the pair of Doos avatars and even through their destruction.

Where were Dr. Acorns and Potato? Seventeen Box remained on Titan's spaceport, determined to abduct them. Was Cooper's plan in play? Would it be effective? Two humans had done what a planet full of Clusterans had not: confronted and defeated Doos. It was inconceivable, yet it had happened. He gazed at the girl as he tried to reconcile the impossible and waited for the hotel doctor to arrive.

CHAPTER FIFTEEN

Back in the main corridors of the spaceport, Coop opened the pillowcase of human and alien hair. He took a small pinch of Potato's blue and green fur and another of Jess's flame-red hair, dropping bits of them here and there as he walked. He continued this practice at every intersection and even tossed some into a passing robotic wagon. He followed Dyrk's directions through the throngs of people.

"This should drive the Box crazy. I like that. A lot."

«That's the idea, but this is just the start. We need to up our game, and I know just the place. Hang a left at the next intersection,» Dyrk instructed.

Coop complied and found himself in a narrow alley between buildings.

"Where are we going?"

«Down. Through that door on the left.»

"Got it." Coop entered the door and descended a metal staircase. After three stories, the stairs ended, and he exited into another corridor. This one was tall. The walls rose up to the equivalent of half the space he'd covered when he came down the stairs. The chamber was packed from floor to ceiling with ducts and pipes and other metalwork required to move air and water through the spaceport at industrial levels.

«There are three main air-control facilities. They detoxify the air and distribute it to the entire spaceport. This was the nearest access point to our location, and it's also the closest to the Box at the departure terminal. Stop here. I need to take over.»

Coop sighed. "Okay."

Dyrk cracked his neck and stretched his arms after he assumed control of Coop's body. He looked around before looking up.

«Just what I was looking for,» he noted in satisfaction.

Dyrk climbed, jumped, and swung his way up the industrial jungle-gym like a ninja doing parkour in his sleep.

Within seconds, he achieved a perch atop the ductwork summit next to a large vent set into the concrete wall. With a few twists, he had the vent's cover removed and propped against the wall.

Dyrk crawled inside and pulled the cover back in place.

That was easy.

«That wasn't the hard part. This is just a branch that will take us to the central facility. That place is pretty well guarded, according to the data I read. I think we can avoid most of the guards by coming in like this.»

You think?

«It isn't like I have much experience with these things. In the movies, the hero always makes it through or meets up with a plot complication to raise the stakes and make his inevitable victory even more satisfying. The thing is, I don't have a script of what's going to happen here.»

I wish you'd stop reminding me of that after *you take control of my body.*

Dyrk chuckled again and crawled along the pitch-black confines of the duct.

I can't see a thing. Can you tell where we're going?

Dyrk had taken out the comm device that Al had given them and aimed the glow of its tiny screen forward. «Huh. I thought this would provide more illumination. No problem. I have a rough idea of where we need to be. We'll be fine.»

A moment later, he banged headfirst into a metal wall.

Miss a turn?

Dyrk sighed. «Hold on, Ben, this may hurt.»

Hurt? More than giving me a concussion? What are you doing?

Without warning, Dyrk was gone, leaving Coop in control of his body, on hands and knees in the dark duct.

"Dyrk?"

«It's easier for me to make adjustments to your body if I'm not running it.»

"Adjustments? What kind of...Arrghhhh!"

Coop clutched at his eyes. There was a brief and intense sensation deep inside them, not quite burning, more like what he imagined it would feel like if bees had somehow gotten inside his eye sockets and were attempting to sting their way back out. Then the sensation passed, though the memory of it lingered. He lowered his hand and found he could see. Not well, but now the light from the comm unit gave an adequate view of the ductwork all around, revealing that Dyrk hadn't reached a dead end, but rather a T-intersection. They had to turn left or right.

"What did you do?"

«Cat eyes.»

"What?!"

«Relax, not actual cat eyes, but the same idea. The part of your eyes that does the seeing, the retina, has two kinds of cells, right? Rods and cones. Cones see color, and rods are better at detecting light. Human eyes have about four times as many rods as cones. Cats have twenty-

five times as many rods as cones. That's why they're so good at seeing in the dark, but not so much when it comes to color discrimination.»

"But what did you *do?*"

«I converted a bunch of your cones to rods. Don't worry. I'll switch them back after we get where we're going. Now, let's swap again.»

Muttering about unsolicited mutations, Coop relaxed and took a mental step back. A moment later, Dyrk had them crawling down the left-hand length of the duct.

After several yards, the wind inside picked up and the ambient noise increased dramatically.

«We're getting close.»

Dyrk crawled a few more yards into another intersection. To his right, the duct widened before ending at a massive fan that was forcing air past him with consistent, solid force. To his left, the duct continued into darkness. A few feet ahead, he saw a trapdoor in the floor. He turned left and stopped to examine a gate leading down and out of the duct. Inset into the face of it was a handle that appeared to be unlocked.

It was right where the schematics said it would be.

With surprising caution and slowness, Dyrk turned the handle and pulled against it, allowing a crack of light to enter the dim confines of the air-tunnel. He leaned closer and pressed his eye against the opening.

He couldn't see much.

There was a concrete floor some twenty feet below him, and more metal pipes cut across his vision, obscuring what little his peek could show him.

«Wish us luck.»

What? Why? Wait!

«Shh, I got this, Ben.»

He opened the hatch all the way. After waiting a moment to see if anyone noticed, he lowered his head through it and looked around.

Nobody screamed or shot at him. Dyrk viewed that as a good sign.

The part of the room he could see contained three things. First, it had a lot of big pipes. Second, there was a far wall, most of it blocked from view, that sounded like a great big fan operated in it. Last, a bored-looking security guard sat at a desk several feet away from Dyrk's preferred landing zone.

«This will be interesting,» he whispered, tucking the pillowcase inside his shirt

You're going to jump down there and attack that guy, aren't you?

«No. I'm going to drop, not jump.»

When did you become a grammar nazi?

Dyrk didn't bother to respond. He was in the zone. Just like that, he lowered himself out of the trapdoor, extended his body to the full extent of his reach, and dropped.

His feet hit the floor, and Dyrk rolled to his right to absorb the impact, then bounded to his feet like a cat, knees bent. He straightened to his full height and placed his hands on his hips in what he believed was an appropriate and dramatic fashion.

Sadly, the security guard didn't seem impressed. Surprised, but not impressed.

What are you doing? Don't stand there posing. Karate chop him already!

Dyrk was a little surprised by Coop's lack of appreciation for his dramatic entrance. Meanwhile, the guard had recovered and reached for a stun baton that sat atop the desk.

That was a problem.

«Fine, Coop. We'll do it your way.»

Dyrk made a blade of his right hand and lashed out with a blow to the man's neck.

The guard stumbled and fell face-first onto the desk. He hadn't been knocked out, and he bravely planted his hands and pushed against the desk to rise.

«Not today, buddy. Go to sleep.»

Dyrk grabbed the man's neck. He applied the appropriate pressure to the proper nerve and counted to five. The guard's body went limp and slumped across his desk.

Dyrk wiped his hands on his trousers and turned to survey the facility.

He was greeted by the shocked expressions of a trio of arriving security guards.

They had just walked in with cups of coffee in their hands, and they gaped at the sight of Dyrk and their unconscious coworker.

Three cups of coffee hit the floor.

The guards drew their stun batons and charged as one.

The confines of the room made it difficult to maneuver—the facility's floor was crowded with pipes and vents running every which way. Dyrk's ultimate goal was the fan on the far side of the room, so he chose the obvious route.

Dyrk went up.

He jumped into the air and grabbed onto a pipe. With one hand, he pulled himself up, then curled his legs and used his coiled energy to launch himself higher. He was just able to grab a support beam with his fingertips.

A stun baton smacked the wall right where his feet had been a moment before.

The sound of the electrical shock could be heard amid the drowning din of the machinery.

Whoa! That guy's baton is a lot stronger than the other ones we've seen.

«Coop, remember when I said I wanted to experience everything?»

Do not *get electrocuted.*

«I'll do my best.»

Dyrk planted his feet against the wall and launched himself into the air again.

En route, he flipped over and executed a perfect twist before landing behind one of the amazed guards.

Dyrk grabbed the man's arm—the one holding the stun baton —at the wrist. He yanked and twisted with savage force. The man yelped, and the baton clattered to the floor. The action hero lashed out with a swift kick to the man's shin to distract him, then reversed his hold and flipped the guard over with a single, fluid movement. He placed his hand on the back of his opponent's head and pressed down. At the same time, Dyrk drove his leg up.

Knee met nose with a crunch.

Dyrk dropped his opponent to the floor. The guard did not get up, but the fight was far from over.

A second guard rushed at Dyrk from his right. The man had his baton extended with the nasty end leading the way.

A flick of the guard's wrist triggered a defensive response, and Dyrk ducked. A bolt of electricity blasted from the baton and over his head. The guard continued forward, and Dyrk narrowly dodged the man's vicious backswing.

He bent over backward and used his momentum to spring into a handstand while the guard's forward motion carried him past Dyrk.

Dyrk dropped back to his feet and hopped on the guard's back.

The man stopped his swing to instead sweep his arm back around at waist height.

There was no way Dyrk was going to avoid the impact if he stayed where he was, so he dropped and pushed hard against the side of the guard's knee. He was rewarded when he felt the kneecap shift.

The guard yelled and fell right on top of Dyrk, but the action hero was ready.

He pummeled the man with a series of punches to his abdomen. He needed to create some distance, so he covered himself with his arms and rolled away. The man stood, flinching because of his knee.

Dyrk kicked him in the side of that knee. The guard screamed and fell back on his ass, clutching his leg.

Dyrk came up on his own knee and pivoted his hips to bring all his force into a strike at the man's jaw, and he went down like it was made of glass, unconscious.

At least he's not feeling the pain of his dislocated kneecap.

Dyrk ignored Ben's comment and came back to his feet. There was still another guard to deal with. He looked around, but the man was nowhere to be found.

Dyrk, he must have run for help. You need to hurry.

«Roger that, Ben.»

Dyrk ran the length of the room to the large turbine spinning inside the opposite wall. He skidded to an abrupt halt when he realized a glass shield stood between himself and the machinery.

«That's inconvenient.»

Over on the right. There's an access panel.

«Thanks, good catch.»

He moved to his right and flipped the latches on the panel. Seconds later, the shield slid open and he felt the air being sucked through the opening. The pull was strong, but not enough to be a danger or risk dragging Dyrk off his feet.

Dyrk pulled the pillowcase from his shirt and reached inside for a handful of Potato's fur, which he let escape between his fingers. The wind pulled it away and he watched it disappear throughout the giant tunnel. He reached in for more fur and hair, repeating the process, all but emptying the pillowcase.

«That should do it,» Dyrk remarked. He folded the bag and returned it to within his shirt.

Good. Now get the hell out of here before that guard comes back with reinforcements.

Dyrk turned to comply and raced back across the room, pausing to help himself to one of the guards' stun batons.

«Do you see that cap on the end?» Dyrk asked. «That's an add-on that's supposed to be limited to military police. It ramps up the power and gives the baton a bit of distance.»

That's how we almost got zapped?

«Pretty much. Only one of them came within range, and I got lucky,» Dyrk explained.

Why don't we have that doodad on our batons?

Dyrk shrugged. «I knew the flaw I'd found in the Box's avatars could be exploited using a standard baton with direct contact. I couldn't tell if it would work at higher power or from a distance. I went with the sure thing.»

It's hard to argue with your results. You wiped out every Box on Titan, before Doos showed up.

«Thanks, I appreciate that.» Holding the rod of the baton with one hand, he began twisting the piece on the end until it popped off. He slipped it into a pocket.

Great. Show that appreciation by getting us the hell out of here. Now.

The route they'd come in was no good. The remaining guard must have spotted the dangling trapdoor. They'd have to leave through the outer office and one of its exits into the spaceport.

Cautiously, Dyrk approached the door he imagined the guard had fled through.

He pressed his ear against it. He heard nothing, so he opened the door. The room beyond was empty save for a couple of chairs, a few desks, and a coffee pot.

Go!

Dyrk did as Coop instructed. He rushed through the room, out its lone door, and found himself face-to-face with the guard who had run away. He wasn't holding a stun baton anymore.

Now he was holding a bolt-pistol.

Dyrk plastered a smile on his face. «Now, that seems unnecessary,» he assured the guard. He closed the door behind him and held his hands up in obvious surrender.

The guard, a young man not yet out of his teens, didn't seem inclined to agree. He jerked the weapon toward Dyrk. His hands shook on the pistol's grip.

«Is this your first job? You seem kind of young for this type of work. Believe me. You can put that gun away. There is no need. I don't want anybody to get hurt. Least of all me, but including yourself.» He took another slow step forward.

"Bullshit. You attacked us. You're…you're a terrorist!"

«Son, I don't have time to explain how wrong you are. Now, if you don't mind, I'm going to walk out that door and never bother you again.»

"Too late. I already called the cops. They said to hold you here." The man seemed a little more confident.

Dyrk took another step. The guard was a few feet away and still had the pistol trained on Dyrk's face.

Dyrk frowned. «That wasn't very hospitable. You see, the police and I are well acquainted. I don't have time for them right now. So, I'm just going to…» Dyrk bent over and ducked his head, then plowed straight into the young man, driving his shoulder into the kid's gut and shoving him all the way across the room until he slammed him into the opposite wall.

The guard lost his wind and his pistol at the same time. In the next instant, Dyrk pushed up with his knees and slammed the top of his head into the underside of the man's jaw.

A stunned look crossed the young man's face right before his eyes rolled into the back of his head. His skinny legs turned into jelly and he crumpled to the floor.

Dyrk brushed his hands off, straightened his shirt, and walked nonchalantly from the office into the corridor beyond.

He had already made two turns and melted into a crowd near a dry goods store by the time the sound of rushing footsteps announced that the police had arrived.

Dyrk whistled to himself and set off on his next task.

CHAPTER SIXTEEN

After things calmed down, Coop took back control of his body.

"I'm hungry. All this fighting is exhausting."

«But I do all the work.»

"It's the same body. It doesn't seem to care who pulls the levers. It just wants food."

He located a restaurant that was little more than a tiny grill on the sidewalk. It had a smattering of mismatched chairs, and mid-sized overturned industrial cable spools served as tables. The aroma of sizzling meat stopped Coop in his tracks. It smelled amazing, and for some inexplicable reason it reminded him of waking up in his trailer with the script girl on the set of *Raining Over Lawyers*. Good times.

The grill's proprietor had opted to make life easy for both himself and his customers. He offered a single product: a generous portion of savory meat dripping with its own juice on a wooden skewer.

"I'll take one," Coop signaled.

«Make it two. It could be a long day.»

Coop shrugged. Dyrk had a point.

"Make it two, please."

The man handed over a pair of meat-laden skewers and a single ironic napkin. Coop took them, paid the man, and smiled. He settled onto a rickety plastic chair and tore into his food.

"Who knew being an action hero could make you so hungry?"

«*Me.*»

"Do you get hungry?"

«*Yes. Maybe worse than you do. Remember, I am hard-wired into your sensory system. What you feel, I feel, and with fewer distractions.*»

"Huh. I hadn't thought about it like that."

«*Ben, can I share something with you?*»

The actor shrugged. "If not with me, then with who, er whom?"

«*You have to promise you won't laugh.*»

"Nope, that's not going to happen."

«*So you won't laugh?*»

"No, I won't promise. We'll just have to see how it goes. Say what you have to say."

In his mind, Dyrk sighed. «*When this is all over, I want to learn how to cook.*»

"What? Why?"

«*It's so primal. So basic and very far outside my experience. Do you know how few of the films that make up my understanding of the world even included enjoying a full meal, let alone preparing one? Less than two percent.*»

"Yeah, that's just the genre. People who go to see action heroes are looking for car chases and explosions, not a ten-course tasting menu at a Michelin star restaurant."

«*No, I get that. It's all the more reason for me to learn to cook. I want to develop my palate. I want to experience everything there is for me to taste.*»

Coop nodded, respecting the sentiment. He took another bite from his skewer. "Okay, well, I'm not laughing. I think that's a pretty good goal."

«*Thank you.*»

"So, tell me. How does this meat taste?"

«Like heaven. You know, a few days ago, everything was so new that it was overwhelming. The tastes were so powerful that I couldn't tell them apart. Now I can appreciate them more. This stuff is amazing.»

"I agree. You should know, where I come from, there are a lot of vegetarians."

«Why? Is meat too expensive? Did all the cows die? Don't they know what they're missing?»

"Don't ask me to explain it, Dyrk. Some things can't be understood. If I've learned anything in this life, it's that you have to respect other people's differences."

«Because we're all unique individuals and everyone's views are valid?»

"Ummm... maybe, but I was thinking because it just makes it easier to get along. Life's too short to spend time arguing about the morality of putting mayonnaise on your french fries."

«Please tell me you're making that up.»

"I wish I was. It's a thing in the Netherlands."

In his head, Coop heard Dyrk shuddering.

Having finished his first meat skewer, Coop appreciated Dyrk's insistence on buying a second. He bit down on a chunk of meat and ripped it from the stick. "Okay, let's get back on track. Where are we going next?"

«We need to head to the terminal and find a ticketing agent of some kind. They should be able to make us a deal on renting a cabin.»

Coop nodded. He knew the way to the terminal, so as soon as he finished skewer number two, he headed in that direction. He wasn't hurried. He took his time, dabbing at the corners of his mouth with the paper napkin as he walked. The meat—whatever kind of meat it had been—had tasted delicious. He wanted to savor it for himself and for Dyrk. Somehow, it felt better knowing that he was sharing the experience. He allowed himself to bask in the experience of the flavors so that his viral co-pilot could do so as well.

Besides, he needed to distribute the remaining bits of Potato's fur, which he accomplished along the way.

Coop left hair at every intersection and made a point of putting some on the many small vehicles that traveled around the port delivering goods and people to their destinations.

Anything he could think of to make things more difficult for the Box bastards seemed like a good idea.

"I hope they lose their little alien minds chasing this stuff around."

Inside his head, Dyrk snickered. Then they arrived at the terminal, and it was time to pay attention.

Just inside the big hall, Coop stopped and stepped out of the crowd to stand against the wall. He looked around for signs of trouble.

"Do you see the Box anywhere?"

«Al said they were at the major exits. I assume he meant to the spaceport itself. So, if they're here, they wouldn't be at the ticketing area. They'd be near the choke points, like heading into security or the passenger terminal for arrivals or the big airlocks where commercial vehicles get loaded and unloaded.»

"That makes sense. All right, let's see what we have here."

Coop looked up and down the ticketing counters. A swarming host of humans and aliens milled about arranging transactions. Porters and laborers came and went with luggage and cargo destined for Earth, other system moons, or, on rarer occasions, the far reaches of the galaxy. It was a busy place. Like an ant colony, but with body odor.

Finally, he found what he needed. A short, bored-looking woman manned a counter underneath a sign for Kuiper Flights that advertised passenger trips to several destinations throughout the solar system. Underneath that sign, a digital message flashed: *All Flights Canceled Due to Repairs.*

"Perfect."

Coop checked the area for any stray Box one last time. Finding none, he moseyed to the counter.

The woman, a middle-aged brunette with an incredible resting-bitch face, glared at him as he approached. Her name tag read "Doris."

"Sorry, we aren't selling tickets right now. All flights are canceled, and we don't know when they'll pick up again."

Coop smiled. "So, you have a great big ship sitting on the ground with nobody on it and no revenue coming in. Am I correct?"

Doris nodded. "You got it, darling. So stop wasting my time."

"Doris, I assure you, that's the last thing I want to do. It just so happens that a fallow starship is the exact thing I'm looking for. I need a private room for a couple of days."

"Then get a hotel room."

"I need more privacy than that. I want to get off-grid, so to speak."

Doris popped the piece of gum in her mouth. "Why? You running from somebody?"

"Does it matter?"

"Not so much. I'm just nosey."

"Noted. So tell me, do you have a passenger room I can rent?"

"I might. I need to know what you're gonna do with the room. This kinda thing can be done, but the last guy who rented it snuck out a day early, and we had to clean lubricants off the ceiling for most of a week. He left a set of manacles bolted into the wall that required an engineer to remove them without further damage, and that wasn't cheap. Then he stiffed us on half of his bill."

"Lubricants? Manacles?"

"Yeah. The pleasure variety, if you get my meaning."

Coop did. He didn't feel like having that conversation with Doris.

"There won't be any of that going on. Two of my friends and I just want to get away. One of my friends is sick, and we want a quiet place for her to recover while we wait for our flight."

"I guess that can be arranged. You'll have to pay up front. Manacle-boy ruined that for everyone."

Coop shook his head to clear away the imagery. "That won't be a problem, Doris. Thank you for all your help."

CHAPTER SEVENTEEN

Al had remained at the bedside of the comatose girl until the house doctor arrived, then lingered only long enough to pass along instructions to do anything and everything possible to see to her comfort and well-being and to contact him if there were any changes. Given his understanding that the girl had been in an unconscious state for months, he didn't deem that to be likely.

Doug, one of his most trusted and useful minions, arrived as Al exited the suite. The crime lord spared him a brief nod. Doug had his instructions. There was nothing more to say to him. Al found himself distracted in ways he had never known before.

All the way back to his underground sanctum, Alhiz'khlo'-tam's thoughts were awhirl. An absolute fact, a fundamental law of reality, had exploded. Doos, the one being who, since the near annihilation of Al's people, had represented all that was evil and implacable in the universe. At the core of his being, Al understood Doos to be as invincible and undefeatable as a force of nature. One might have better luck attempting to confront a hurricane.

This was why, since gaining power and influence on Titan, he had fought back against the Box in indirect ways. He had interfered with their shipments, hacked their communications satellite, reverse engineered their technology, and put it out on the open market. He had never come at any of them directly—Doos' destruction of Clustera had demonstrated the futility of that—but he had annoyed and distracted and hindered them from the shadows at every turn.

He'd had opportunity to study eight distinct Box personae, and while they had varied significantly, they shared a common, algorithmic world view. This had befuddled and confounded him at first. Such an approach was the antithesis of how all Clusterans understood life. His people were spontaneous, creative, and unpredictable. They progressed through inspiration and random moments of illumination. They had been nothing like the Box, which Al believed had contributed to their doom. Since coming to Titan, he had damped these attributes and learned to recognize and understand the cold and logic-based perspective of the Box. It was a matter of knowing his enemy, a foe who could be endlessly harassed if never actually defeated.

Except apparently, they *could* be defeated.

Mere days ago, Cooper had rid Titan of every active Box extension belonging to the three distinct individuals who had been here. Earlier today, he had physically beaten Doos, a complete and utter impossibility. And more recently still, it appeared that perhaps Dr. Acorns had taken the impossible to a greater level by vanquishing two instantiations of Doos.

A fundamental concept of the universe had changed. Doos was not invincible.

He needed to check on his daughter first. She remained his greatest priority, no matter what else might happen. He paused to consult the status of the remaining Doos extensions on Titan. The majority remained at the spaceport's entry points, the same as they'd been earlier, and the few avatars that roamed the streets appeared to move about randomly. The data suggested they had not abducted Dr. Acorns nor secured Potato. Everything was still in play, which in turn meant he had much to do. It would all wait long enough for him to see Antella'nestra, though.

He found her as he had left her, focused on her work, guiding the sonic loom in the intricate construction of another colandracel. At the farthest edge of her worktable, he saw evidence that she had eaten a meal. Judging by the clothing in the 'fresher, she had changed into a clean outfit, even showered or bathed. He checked the memory of the room's multi-purpose exercise device and found she had completed a mini workout. All these things assured him that Antella'nestra continued to tend to the necessities of life, even if she allotted the barest minimum time to them, even if she never spoke or showed interest in anything beyond the growing and shaping of her crystals.

"Daughter, the universe has changed," he murmured, stepping behind her and placing a hand on her shoulder. The touch was the merest contact. Any more, and she might perceive it as interfering with her work and shrug him off. He needed that contact, ephemeral as it may be.

"For the first time since we lost everything, I feel a possibility of hope. I can envision a day when I would play the colandracel again."

His daughter said nothing,

"Mind you, I do not say that I can take up the instrument at this time, but the possibility is now in my mind and heart. So many things now seem possible, sweet one. Perhaps even, one day, you will be returned to me, whole and reborn. Another impossibility that today I am able to question."

He turned from her. If the impossible was now possible, many new strategies and tactics likewise came into existence. Doubtless, many—perhaps even most—would fail. He could not know for sure until he explored them.

Al stepped into the pawnshop and gazed with undisguised distaste at the intersection of cacophony, visual blight, and faint but unmistakable blend of the vast variety of stench humans were capable of producing. The Clusteran sensorium covered a wider range and possessed greater sensitivity than that enjoyed by Titan's majority population, whom he sometimes suspected were quite content to live in their own swill. That seemed to be the case of the pawnshop's proprietor, a self-important weasel of a man with whom Al had the misfortune to have done business recently. This, too, was something that Cooper had caused.

The object of his contempt emerged from an entrance behind the shop's overflowing counter, his arms full of more secondhand merchandise that he was attempting to force on top of other worthless treasures on the counter. He spoke as he did this, still not looking at his potential customer, only having been alerted that someone had entered the shop.

"What may I help you with today?" asked Patel. "Be assured, my friend, I will offer top dollar on whatever you have to show me, or make you the best of possible bargains on anything in my stock that you wish to acquire."

Al cleared his throat, and the pawnbroker looked up. Patel blanched. The merchandise he'd carried in from the back room fell from his hands, causing other items to tumble from the countertop in turn.

"Al…how can I be of assistance to you?"

"You can begin by never mistaking to call me 'friend' ever again."

"Of course, sir."

The crime boss stared at Patel, his gaze pinning the much smaller man like a hobbyist would pin a bug with a sharp implement driven through the abdomen.

"I am in need of a human appliance. I do not know what it is called."

"An appliance?"

"Several. They are programmable, semiautonomous cleaning devices for floors."

Patel frowned, struggling to make sense of the words.

"You mean...a Roomba?"

Al stepped to the counter and slammed it. "I already told you I do not know its name. Do you have such a thing in your stock? Bring it to me, and I will know if we are talking about the same object."

The pawnbroker took the instruction as a welcome excuse to flee into the back room.

Al sighed and examined his comm unit. He suspected Patel would be a while. Fortunately, he was an expert at multitasking. He made a call.

"Doug! Have you completed your task?"

"Yes, sir. I'm arriving at Warehouse #3 now. It's taken a bit longer than I'd anticipated. There's a fierce dust storm hanging over the warehouse district, making traffic between it and the spaceport kinda tricky. I've called ahead, and a crew is waiting to empty the van once I arrive."

"Very good. Delegate the completion of that task to someone else. I need you to go to Warehouse #5 and locate some thermite for me."

"Did you say 'thermite,' boss?"

"Yes. I'd like fifteen shaped charges capable of being triggered by a simple electric signal. Each should have a fixative on the underside to permit it to be mounted on an otherwise slick surface."

"Copy that. I'm certain I can cobble something together. How soon do you need them?"

"Yesterday. Linear time is the least of my concerns. I intend to do the impossible."

"I'll do my best. Anything else?"

"When you have them ready, bring them in through commercial transit gate seven."

"You sure, boss? That's one of the entry points with a Box standing around scanning everyone who goes in or out."

"Absolutely. I'll meet you inside the airlock and take delivery. You won't have to go near the Box."

Patel came back into the shop's main room at that moment, carrying three variations of metallic disks, each the diameter of a dinner plate and a hand or so high. Al ended the call.

"Is this what you meant?"

Al nodded. "I believe so. Are their movements programmable?"

"Completely. A child could do it."

The Clusteran glared but let the unintended slur pass. "I need fifteen of them. Different makes and models are fine so long as they all are capable of predetermined locomotion."

"I have these three, but..." He flinched and added, "Let me call around. I'm sure I can lay my hands on some more units. Maybe not another dozen, but I should be able to come close."

"Then that will have to suffice. I strongly encourage you to make every effort. Acquire as many as you can over the next hour, then deliver them to commercial transit gate seven. I'll take receipt of them there. Patel, do not fail me in this."

"Of course not, Al. You know you can depend on me."

"Can I? Hmm, I would not have thought so, but the impossible has become possible today."

Patel shook his head. "I don't understand."

"Then let me phrase it in a manner that has more meaning for you. You recall that your family owes me a large debt."

"Yes, sir."

"My need for these things is so great that if you can succeed at this task, get me what I need when I need it, I will erase that debt like it never existed. The impossible made possible."

Patel's eyes went wide. He set the three Roombas on the floor, nodding frantically. "Excuse me, Al. I'll get on this immediately."

Alhiz'khlo'tam, one of three crime bosses who had divided all questionable activity on Titan, turned and exited the pawnshop. Behind him, Patel was already on the comm, reaching out in search of another twelve devices.

CHAPTER EIGHTEEN

Jessica's eyes opened, but only under duress. She needed to awaken, and at some level she knew it. There were...things, surely, that she needed to be doing, though in this moment she couldn't remember what they might be, and she didn't want to remember. Just the thought of moving or standing, even breathing, made her head hurt. She'd had enough pain for two lifetimes. She didn't want to feel that kind of torment ever again, but she continued to breathe anyway. The agony didn't arrive as anticipated. Its specter lingered in her mind, taunting her until she felt she had no choice but to face it down. She forced herself into a sitting position.

She was on the bed-turned-examination table in her makeshift lab in their hotel suite. That was good. It was important to know where you were, to be grounded like that. Everything else seemed...wrong. Her body felt weird. Things looked different, like they were...off, somehow. The whole world swam when she stood. Nothing moved like it should. Everything seemed out of place. It was like she lived in a room full of funhouse mirrors without the fun.

"Whoa, whoa, are you okay, miss?"

A kindly-looking older man in a cardigan and worn denim jeans appeared in the doorway. His face was a map of wrinkles, including deep-set laugh lines. He wore a bow tie. The ends of a stethoscope dangled over his sweater on either side of his neck.

"It's Doctor, Doctor."

"Sorry?"

"I'm Dr. Acorns. Who are you?"

"Most people just call me Eddy. I'm the hotel's physician, though mostly all I tend to are folks in need of hangover cures. Not you, though. They tell me you've been in a coma for months. Hard to credit though, the way you're moving around."

Coma? Months? What was he talking about?

Eddy advanced into the room. Settling his stethoscope into place, he came closer. "How about we get a listen to your ticker, little lady, and go from there?"

She pushed past him, a bit steadier on her feet. The world still felt off, but the ageism and sexism were familiar. Lurching into the foyer, she saw that someone had hauled away the damaged Box avatar that Mr. Cooper had killed. Someone else had left a trail of bloody footprints coming from one of the other bedrooms.

Jessica froze.

That was the bedroom where she'd left Tycho!

Still unsteady, she staggered across the foyer to the bedroom door, aware of the house physician trailing behind.

She peered into the bedroom and gaped at the destruction.

"What the hell happened? And how did I miss it?"

She racked her brain. Glass littered the floor. Bullet holes decorated one wall, and the smell of smoke—which explained the scorch marks—still hung around. A massive hole in the opposite wall provided a view into the bathroom beyond, which also looked to have been shot up. Soaking in the full extent of the destruction, it came back to her.

"Oh shit, the Box!"

Memories burst into her awareness. Doos had returned. Two of it. With...what had Dyrk called it, a fear gun?

She turned and saw the empty bed. "Tycho! No! And where's Potato? Oh, no. No, no, no..."

Jessica searched for her tablet. Scanning her surroundings, she found it on the floor nearby. She crossed to it, reached for it, but missed it by an inch.

What the hell? Did I take a hit to the head?

"Please, miss. Why don't you sit down before you hurt yourself?"

The elderly doctor had followed her into the room. Jessica glared at him and shooed him back into the foyer. Again she regarded her tablet, trying not to think why she'd missed it. She grabbed for it again. Once she had it in her hands, she punched up the comms link for Mr. Cooper. A moment later, his cocky voice came out of the speaker, tinny and annoying.

"Hey, honey..."

"Shut up and listen, Mr. Cooper."

"Ooookay."

"Where are you?"

"We're on our way back. We just left the ticketing terminal about five minutes ago. Everything's set. What's up?"

"I don't know what happened, but a pair of Doos came here. Tycho and Potato are gone. I was unconscious, and I just woke up. Her bedroom is demolished. It looks like a war zone." She sent him a picture from her tablet, showing a view of the bedroom and its new post-apocalyptic aesthetic.

"Whoa."

"Whoa is right. Wait, hold on. There's an emergency notice coming in."

Jessica tapped on the red box flashing at the top of her screen, and an alert jumped to the fore.

WARNING—AVOID THE PASSENGER TERMINAL—TERRORIST ATTACK IN PROGRESS—WARNING

The message repeated, scrolling again across the screen, then an alert for a video feed popped up. She opened it to get a glimpse of the emergency and gasped.

There was Tycho, an alien weapon in each hand, firing on the Box. Potato was perched on her shoulder, clinging to her lithe neck. The Box were shooting back, but seemed to be aiming for her legs. Most of their shots missed, but with so many rounds, a few managed to strike home, doing savage amounts of damage. As Jessica watched, Tycho fell. When she did, the Doos extensions stopped firing—for fear of striking Potato, Jessica suspected.

But that was all the time Tycho needed. The teen rose up, healed to perfection, and resumed her side of the firefight.

Jess returned to her conversation with Mr. Cooper. "It's Tycho. She's awake. Her virus is working. Double overtime! And she's shooting it out with Doos at the main passenger terminal."

"That's great. It would also explain all the screaming people running past us from that direction."

"Great? I don't think so."

"Why not?"

"She's had no real brain function for months. From the look of her, and what I can see on my tablet, the lights are on, but nobody's home."

"That doesn't make any sense. How could she be holding her own against the Box?"

"War movies," explained Jess.

Mr. Cooper was silent for a shocked moment. "Oh, crap. Okay, I'm on my way. Dyrk and I will handle this. Stay put."

"Like hell I will."

CHAPTER NINETEEN

Coop had just left ticketing. He pushed forward, attempting to force his way toward the main passenger terminal. It was like swimming upstream, a lone heroic salmon fighting a tide of humanity and aliens. Worse, it was a tide of panicked sapience, doing everything it could to escape from whatever was happening back at the terminal, screaming and shoving with desperate fear and chaos. This portion of the terminal was lined with shops and vendor kiosks scattered through the middle of the thoroughfare. The sheer press of bodies had knocked down several kiosks. The people were too frightened to do any looting, but the added obstacles caused a lot of cursing and a few punches to be thrown. Amid it all, Coop did his best to advance.

«I'm gonna guess...fear gun.»

Coop snorted. "You think?"

His shoulders were getting sore from all the jostling. Dyrk whisked away the pain the instant it manifested, but even so, it was pissing him off. "Move, dammit!" Coop growled. He shoved his way past one particularly slow and stupid man who had gotten in his way. The guy's cow-like eyes added to the perception of slowness that exuded from him like sludge.

«Coop, maybe I should take over.»

"No, not yet. Bad as this is, whatever is happening at the terminal will be worse. If Doos is painting the crowd with infrasonic terror, you'll need to take over once we get in range. You can't be tiring yourself out now. Besides, I need to put my new body to the test."

«Are you sure?»

"Yeah, Dyrk. I'm sure. Now give me a second to think."

Coop pressed against a kiosk and did his best to let people surge past him. He looked around for an alternative to wading through the crushing throng. He found it ten feet up.

A series of conduit pipes ran the length of the corridor. Four of them were packed together, held aloft by what he hoped were strong braces. They ran the length of the terminal and could deliver him to his destination. He just needed a way up.

Looking around, he pushed a crazed-looking xenon from him and ran four steps to his left, where he jumped on a robotic cart that had been turned on its side.

Step one, he thought.

Coop leapt and grabbed the metal support of an awning that hung over a consignment shop before doing three-quarters of a pull-up.

"Ha! I still got it!"

«More like you've got it again. You haven't been able to do a move like that in more than twenty years.»

Coop opted to ignore Dyrk, focusing on the task at hand.

Step two. One left.

The actor pulled his knees up, planted them on the bar he'd used to leverage himself above the awning, and jumped straight up and out over the crowd. He reached the pipes without effort—in fact, he overshot and slammed his chest against them.

"Ouch." He pulled the rest of his body onto the conduits.

Coop saw a small, blue-skinned alien staring at him. The little xenon overcame its fear and clapped politely. Then it got trampled as another wave of people came rushing through the hall.

"Ouch again." Coop shrugged and pulled himself to his feet. He couldn't stand upright, but he got straight enough to manage a slow, half-hunched jog toward the other end of the terminal. The pipes provided an excellent track for him to follow. In a short time, the business end of the spaceport where passengers boarded shuttles came into view.

It was also about that time that he began to hear gunshots, a lot of them.

"That's not good. It's got to be Doos. No one else would be stupid enough to use projectile weapons in the spaceport, not even the sorry excuse for a police force here."

«We've already seen the Box don't understand tactics. It's going to kill someone, maybe a lot of someones. Can't you move this thing any faster?»

"This *thing* is me. It is my body. Maybe I can. I haven't tried."

Coop pushed his legs harder and was pleased to find he did have a higher gear, even bent over as he was.

His personal runway came to an end at the intersection where new arrivals could turn right in pursuit of their luggage or left to arrange for ground transportation to the buildings outside the spaceport proper. Coop didn't waste time. He looked, he jumped, he grabbed onto a lower pipe and swung himself to a cleared area right behind a mass of milling police officers. He landed with a proud, self-satisfied smile on his face.

"That was cool."

«I give it a six, tops.»

"Nobody asked you."

The cops were overwhelmed. Some tried to push their way into the terminal. Others were trying to get more people out of the terminal. Some of the panicked civilians punched and pushed the cops trying to help them. A few officers resorted to tossing grenades of a sleeping agent into some of the more unruly packs.

"That's one way to keep them from trampling each other to death."

«Whatever is happening with Tycho is happening farther in. Get a move on.»

Dyrk was right. Coop began dodging and weaving, using his enhanced agility and reduced waistline to wend his way through the crowds. One officer in a gas mask turned and instinctively tried to push Coop back. Just as instinctively, Coop punched him in the face.

The cop collapsed like a sack of potatoes, and a grenade of some sort fell from his grasp.

«That guy looked familiar.»

"Did he? I've punched so many cops in the last week that they're all looking the same to me."

«You mean limp and unconscious?»

"Well, yeah."

The grenade rolled to a stop at his feet. Coop saw its pin had remained in place.

He grabbed the grenade and stuffed it into a pocket. "Waste not, want not."

He ran at the phalanx of police officers ahead of him. They were focused on whatever was happening on the other side and had their backs to him. It was a simple matter to use one of their backs as a springboard to dive up and over their shoulders, then past them. He landed, rolled, and rode the momentum to his feet. He stood in a small clearing. The cops he'd jumped over like so many pieces in a game of checkers had been holding a line, letting panicked civilians through until it was just cops, more cops, Box extensions, and somewhere past everything else, Tycho.

"We've got to be getting near the range of Doos' fear gun," stated Coop. "I don't see any cops beyond here. Maybe they've figured out the distance by trial and error."

«Get as close as you can. I'm ready to move the moment I detect the

first tingle of fear.»

Nodding to himself, the actor strode ahead. Things did not look good.

He saw Tycho. She stood at the end of the terminal. The Doos had her backed into a corner, and she appeared to be using an overturned cart and its erstwhile luggage as cover. That wasn't going to be enough.

Potato still clung to the young woman. Tycho had just stood again. Her legs looked a bit unsteady, but the weapon clutched in her hands seemed fine.

Fanned out around her at a respectful distance were nine Box extensions. Like the one Dyrk had fought earlier, they were all armed to the teeth with an assortment of weapon limbs, most of which could do a lot more damage than mere bullets. They had no interest or concern for the cops holding the perimeter behind them. They were an avenging horde, and Tycho was their sole focus. Nine against one. The odds sucked.

A handful of police stood between Coop and the Doos. The cops looked less focused, but one of them, a negotiator of some sort, had positioned himself off to one side, closer to the action than any of the other cops. He crouched behind a pillar. He had a bullhorn, and he wasn't afraid to use it.

"Surrender now. You are in violation of multiple spaceport ordinances. Put down your weapons before someone gets hurt."

Coop looked around the terminal skeptically. He noted the presence of many unconscious bodies. Some were bruised and bloody from being trampled.

«Is this guy serious?»

"I bet he thinks he is."

Coop turned his gaze back to Tycho in time to watch her pop up and unleash a burst of lightning bolt rounds at one of the Doos. The avatar had tried to flank her and received three perfect shots to its carapace for its efforts. The Box withdrew, slumping before it rolled to a halt, its internal mechanisms fried. One down, eight to go.

But it had been a feint. During the distraction, another Doos had taken aim and fired one of its weapons at Tycho. The kinetic round smashed into the girl's leg. Her knee skewed sideways in a way that knees are not meant to skew, and Tycho dropped like a rock.

The Box closed in. They didn't get far.

Coop stared in awe as the young woman's leg snapped back into place on its own. She jumped back to her feet like nothing had happened and sprayed the Doos avatars with automatic weapons fire. The Box stopped their advance. Some even retreated.

"Geez, did you see how fast she healed?"

Dyrk whistled inside Coop's mind. *«I sure did. Did you see the blank look in her eyes?»*

Coop had. He nodded solemnly. Tycho didn't look human, but her actions weren't random and her fire hadn't been indiscriminate. She'd only sprayed live rounds at the advancing avatars. None of the cops had been hit.

«Coop, maybe you should duck or find cover.»

"Right you are." Coop bent over and rushed behind a pillar.

As he continued to watch, Tycho and a pair of Doos exchanged fire. One of the extensions collapsed in a smoking heap, but the other managed to score a hit. Tycho jerked back, and blood blossomed on her shin. Through it all, Potato maintained its perch atop her shoulder and managed to lick her brow during lulls in the excitement.

"What is that stupid little furball doing?"

«It's lapping up the pheromones she's putting out through her sweat. It can't help itself. I bet it reeks of chemical scents of its own. That's got to be how she's healing so fast.»

"Again with the pheromones?"

«The virus communicates with its host through smell. Potato is the

source of the virus. Ergo—»

"Yeah, yeah, Potato's a stinkpot, I get it."

«Potato may well be the reason Tycho's still alive. The Doos won't aim high for fear of hitting it.»

"That's nice to know, but how do we use it? We need to shut the Box down and stop Tycho from shooting anyone who comes near her. You got any ideas?"

Dyrk didn't get to respond. Several of the cops chose that moment to open fire, ending the brief lull. It jerked Coop's attention back to the fight.

Things went to hell quickly. The police fired a fusillade of non-lethal rounds at the Doos extensions. None of them caused any damage, but the electronic interference they produced got the Box's attention. They now viewed the cops as a threat.

Four of the avatars turned. From his position behind the pillar, Coop fell to his knees, convulsing with inexplicable terror. Dyrk came to the fore and the sensation drained away.

«No worries, Ben, I got this. You okay?»

Coop shuddered deep in his mind. *I will be.*

The police fared worse. Some collapsed, and others turned to flee. It didn't matter. All four of those Box extensions whipped identical weapon limbs into play and aimed gouts of acid at the police.

Dyrk ducked back behind the pillar. Howls of terror turned to screams of agony. He counted to ten as the battle raged across the terminal, then he peeked out again. Several uninjured cops were pulling their injured comrades to safety. Others came to take their place. Some carried shields large enough to provide cover for multiple combatants. Others dropped into position, aiming new and much more lethal-looking weapons at the robotic juggernauts. They didn't intend to be as gentle this time. Unfortunately, their intention failed when they came within range of the fear gun. The same four Doos advanced on the quivering humans, passing Dyrk's position, while their compatriots resumed their fire against Tycho.

The young woman took more hits. She absorbed them. She healed, albeit slower than before. Her recovery rate was flagging.

I don't know how much more of this she can take.

«She's only made it this long because Potato is with her and amping up the virus. It's a fuzzy catalyst for the virus's growth and activation.»

Got it. Potato equals superhuman Tycho. Now, do you have any ideas about how to get them out of here without us getting killed? Because that would be helpful.

Across the battlefield, Tycho popped up from behind some smoldering luggage and managed to hit a Doos square in the chest with a liquid-metal round. The avatar halted, out of commission. The young woman pivoted to her left and walked a string of those same lethal projectiles along the body of another Box, dismembering it into a pile of slag.

«I almost feel bad for them. Almost.»

She took an electric bolt in the hip and disappeared from view behind the Samsonite mountain. A new scent of burned flesh wafted from the luggage.

Dyrk, I know she is...or was, brain dead. I know she was programmed on war movies and post-apocalyptic garbage, but I don't want to see her get killed, either.

«This isn't my specialty, Ben. I understand strategy, make no mistake, but I do my best work with spontaneity and improvisation. It's clear that the Box have two big advantages here. First, they aren't worried about surviving. They only need one extension to make it out of here with Potato. Second, they don't care about anyone else surviving. I think Doos will raze the entire spaceport to get what it wants. Those seem like big factors in favor of it winning. If Al was right and Doos arrived with twenty avatars, there's another ten that will soon be on their way.»

Wait, you're right.

«Am I? About what?»

The Box. There might be more of them coming. We need reinforcements!

«You're excited about this? Just when I thought I understood humans—»

Shut up, Dyrk. Just get ready. You see the guy with the bullhorn? He wasn't affected by the fear gun. Does that mean he's out of its effective field?

«Probably. I don't think it has a very wide arc.»

Great. Go smack him in the head.

«Why?»

Because I need his bullhorn, just for a few seconds to deliver my lines. Then you'll take over again.

Dyrk looked around and focused on his new target. The jackass was lying down, still shouting through his bullhorn. His weapon remained holstered.

Earth cops would eat these guys for breakfast. They're about as effective as the stormtroopers in that first Star Wars movie.

«Classic flick!»

Yeah!

«Okay, here we go.»

Dyrk sprinted out from behind his cover. He crossed the intervening distance in record time. At the last moment, he slid to his knees on the marble flooring of the terminal and allowed his momentum to carry him the rest of the way. He collided with the surprised cop and delivered a sucker punch right to the officer's temple. The man's head jerked and smacked against the pillar he had been hiding behind, and the bullhorn fell from his limp fingers. Dyrk snatched it up.

None of the other cops seemed to have noticed. That, or they didn't care. Which was understandable. They had more important things on their minds.

«Okay, you're up. You remember our common goal?»

Don't get us killed?

«That's the one!»

Dyrk receded into Coop's mind, leaving the actor in control of their shared body. Coop pulled the trigger for the microphone and leaned out, pointing the bullhorn at Tycho.

"HANG IN THERE, SOLDIER! REINFORCEMENTS HAVE ARRIVED! WE'RE COMING FOR YOU!" He followed this with an admirable imitation of a bugle sounding *charge!* then ducked back behind the pillar.

"All right, Dyrk. It's action time. Go get our pretty little war machine."

CHAPTER TWENTY

While anyone who was anyone on Titan maintained a residence or at least an office in the spaceport proper, entrepreneurs and industrialists had taken advantage of the cheaper real estate beyond. An entire warehouse district had grown up a short drive from the spaceport, which in turn had led to the construction of twenty commercial gates at one end of the facility. This had been accomplished by adding a cul-de-sac to the spaceport and spacing the gates out at regular intervals along the resulting arc. Each had airlocks big enough to accommodate a small truck. Seventeen of these were available on a rental basis in two-hour increments and were reserved weeks in advance, around the clock. The remaining gates had been set aside for the exclusive use of the spaceport's three crime bosses.

Alhiz'khlo'tam's was commercial transit gate seven.

He'd left the central location of Patel's pawnshop and set out for the gate. His long legs carried him faster than a pedicab could. Also, he needed to burn off some energy. His brain buzzed with his intentions. It was one thing to all at once plan to do the impossible, but until he implemented the idea, it was only a fanciful dream. It wasn't a dream he wanted to wake from, even as the prospect of living in the resulting world unnerved him.

No one on all of Titan had ever seen Al unnerved, nor imagined it.

He activated his comm as he walked and spoke to another of his minions.

"Clara, if you please, review the status board and tell me the locations of the remaining Box."

After a moment of silence, Clara replied, "I'm showing seventeen of the original twenty, sir."

"That's consistent with my own accounting," agreed Al. "Three of the roving avatars have been disabled. As for the rest, any change to their distribution?"

"Originally, thirteen had set up positions at various entry points throughout the spaceport. Five of those have moved on, and it looks like they've been joined by four remaining rovers, for a total of nine that have converged in the vicinity of the passenger terminal."

"Nine?"

"Yes, sir. I'm getting reports of a riot at the passenger terminal. No, wait. Make that eight Box there. One of the nine just went offline."

A word flitted through Al's mind. *Impossible.* Then it was gone. In its place was the realization that Cooper, and perhaps Dr. Acorns, were at the passenger terminal. No one else on Titan could do the impossible.

Unless he changed that.

"So Doos has eight of its extensions at the passenger terminal and the remaining eight guarding entry points?"

"Yes, sir. Three are at the hub of commercial gates, two more at customs, and the remaining three spread out along the length of the spaceport at the more prominent export portals. We, of course, have full monitoring of the export locations."

"Of course."

The three crime bosses had divided Titan not in terms of territory, but activity. Big Tony held sway over gambling, protection, and general racketeering. The Diamond Queen's domain included drugs, alcohol, and sex work. Al had laid claim to the import and export trade. Each of them had some small instances of overlap, but in the interests of Titanian harmony, the three bosses had always managed to work things out peaceably.

"And sir, I've just received a report about the young woman you'd left in the doctor's care at the presidential suite of the *Palais Titan*."

"What of her?"

"She woke up insisting she was Dr. Jessica Acorns and ran off."

"That makes no sense," noted Al. "The human I left with Eddy was a teenage female with dark hair. Dr. Acorns is a decade older, taller, with red hair. It should be impossible to confuse the two."

"Yes, sir."

Al frowned and tried to understand. Had Dr. Acorns been transformed? And even if she had, what had become of the comatose teen she now resembled? And where was Potato?

"Thank you, Clara. Keep me apprised of any new movements among the Box. I'm nearing the far end of the spaceport now."

Al turned his comm off and approached the hub of the commercial gates. A Doos avatar rolled toward him, its treads ominous and silent.

"Clusteran!"

Al kept his expression neutral. He continued walking, stopping when the other choice was to collide with the Box. He swallowed hard and felt himself sweat. This creature had destroyed his life, his family, his people, and his world.

Impossible. Impossible. Impossible.

"It is rare to encounter a Clusteran," observed Doos.

Al said nothing.

"What brings you here?"

Al gestured toward the arc of commercial gates. "I have business there."

"What kind of business? Does it involve a human physician and researcher?"

"No. I am receiving a shipment of…cleaning devices."

"Cleaning devices?"

Al nodded. Given the vast array of sensors available to Doos, it was safe to assume it was monitoring him, looking for any indication of falsehood. "Semiautonomous cleaning devices."

"And you don't know of any human physician?"

"I believe there was one employed by some of your fellow Box at a compound out beyond the spaceport."

"Yes, that is the one. Do you know where she can be found?"

So she wasn't part of whatever was happening at the passenger terminal, else this Doos would already know it.

"No idea," Al answered truthfully. "With all of your advanced technology, I am surprised you cannot locate her."

"On the contrary, I have located her without difficulty. That is the conundrum."

"How so?"

The Box waved a limb, gesturing with the weapon. "She is… all around, and yet…she is nowhere."

Al bit back his smile. Score another point for Cooper. "Curious. One would think that, given how you distribute your consciousness across multiple avatars, you wouldn't be so puzzled by a human who appears ubiquitous. Now, will you excuse me? As I said, I have business."

"You may go."

Impossible. Impossible. Impossible.

Al wanted nothing more than to fling this and every Doos avatar into the sun with an act of will. He opted to step around this Box and continue walking. He moved into the cul-de-sac of the commercial gates and noted two more avatars, positioned like the foci of an ellipse. They ignored him, doubtless having the report from the one who'd questioned him.

He proceeded to gate seven, where two low piles of hardware had been stacked alongside the entrance. Roombas. Several of Patel's people had already come through and dropped off their wares. None had been concerned about possible theft. Everyone knew who owned gate seven.

The crime boss applied himself to the gate's security panel and entered a code to gain access. The large airlock was empty—Doug hadn't arrived yet but would be on his way. Al carried the devices within. He was still short the expected fifteen units. One of the things he'd learned since arriving on Titan was to have backups. Even so, he no longer had thirteen Box extensions standing guard at the spaceport's entry points. Perhaps more of the cleaning devices would arrive, or he'd have to make do. Backup units or no, he would go forward.

While he waited, Al slipped into a pressure suit he'd had crafted to accommodate his size and reviewed the programming controls for the cleaning devices. As promised, there were several different makes, although they all used similar interfaces. He had mastered the particulars of two types and was well into the third when an alarm sounded and warning lights flashed all around him. Moments later, equipment in the walls sucked the atmosphere from the room, replacing it with the toxic mix from the moon's surface. When that process had completed, the outer gate opened to allow an all-terrain vehicle to roll in. It stopped in front of the crime boss.

Doug had arrived.

The outer door closed. The airlock expelled the Titanian atmosphere with its extra levels of methane and cyanide, replacing it with the terrestrial blend that had been present when Al had entered. The lights stopped flashing, and the vehicle opened to reveal a doughy-looking man in stained coveralls. A name tag stitched on the garment's left breast bore the name 'Doug.' He held a crate in his arms and brought it forward.

"Any problem obtaining the thermite?" asked Al.

"No, sir, nor the fixative. I've got it all right here. I can have the charges good to go as soon as you show me what you want to trigger them."

Al held out one of the cleaning devices. Doug cocked an eyebrow. "A Roomba?"

"Does everyone know about these but me? Never mind, can you do it?"

"Set the Roomba to trigger a charge? Sure. Easy peasy."

"Excellent. At present, you have more thermite than I have devices. More may be coming, or not, but for now, please work with what we have."

Doug set the crate down and took the Roomba from Al. He settled on the floor of the airlock and pulled a multi-tool from a pocket of his overalls, and got to work.

Fifteen minutes later, the inner airlock door of commercial transit gate seven opened, and Alhiz'khlo'tam emerged into the cul-de-sac. He'd checked in with Clara that the eight Box extensions positioned near entry points hadn't moved, and from his position he confirmed the three nearest, two in the arc of gates and a third that had confronted him on the main thoroughfare of the spaceport.

Impossible. Impossible. Impossible.

He put a smile on his face, straightened his clothing, and strode forward, leaving the open airlock of gate seven behind him. His route took him between the two nearest avatars, and he stopped when going any farther would have meant he could only keep one of them in his vision at a time. There were plenty of people around. The other commercial transit gates enjoyed constant usage, and even now, several were open with workers unloading cargo from transports parked within. Others lay empty. Pallets of outbound merchandise and supplies were stacked against the walls, awaiting the arrival of a vehicle to haul them to the warehouse district or some remote building on the moon's surface.

Al waved to them all. He bowed. When he spoke, it was with the strong voice of a man used to being heard, giving orders, and being obeyed. He didn't know what he would say but knew he had to begin.

Impossible. Impossible. Impossible.

"Citizens of Titan! The universe has changed. It happened today. You may not have noticed it—I myself hadn't noticed it at first—but the change was there all the same. Like most monumental changes, it was a small thing, but the significance of it rippled outward throughout the universe, redefining reality."

All around him, people had stopped to stare. Everyone who had business at this end of the spaceport knew which commercial gates belonged to the crime bosses, even if they had no idea who the bosses were or what they looked like. A popular rumor was that one of them was a xenon. Now, here was an ebony giant who had emerged from one of the privileged gates. It didn't take a rocket scientist to work out who he must be. They stopped whatever they were doing and paused to listen.

Doos likely didn't know about crime bosses. Such things were beneath its concern. It did seem to register that the xenon it had questioned had, through the use of oratory, caused a break in the orderly workflow of many humans. Its two closest extensions rotated their torsos to orient their full sensor arrays on him and scan for additional anomalies.

Al noticed, still smiling, and pointed at both avatars.

"So what is this change? How has reality been redefined? Believe me when I say, this is not a rhetorical question. I will tell you the answer. It's simple, quite simple, in fact."

Impossible. Impossible. Impossible.

Like a man standing at the open edge of a spacecraft's airlock gazing at the oblivion beyond, he paused for a moment. There could be no further delay. He'd already committed himself.

"Today, the impossible became possible. That which could never occur has happened. It did not just happen once. Once might be a fluke, an aberration, but repetition, replication, that makes it real. I've seen it with my own eyes, and having seen it, how could I not attempt to achieve the thing myself?"

He slipped a hand into a pants pocket, long fingers finding a small control device Doug had given him. His gaze drifted from one position to another to a third, confirming that three of the programmable cleaning devices had indeed slipped out from the open airlock of gate seven and found their way to the three Box, slipped into the space between their pairs of treads, and parked themselves under their respective torsos.

"Just as I have witnessed this thing firsthand, now you shall too. Behold! The impossible made possible!"

A touch of the control triggered three shaped thermite charges, sending gouts of four-thousand-degree flame into each Doos avatar, burning into them, melting core systems and killing them in an instant.

Despite the focus of the thermite, there was some spillover. The Roombas themselves were reduced to slag, and waves of heat radiated outward from the three explosions. People screamed and ran, some into open gates, others deeper into the spaceport itself. In less than a minute, Al stood there alone.

For a while, he just soaked it in, still disbelieving. He'd raised a hand to the creature that had ended everything that had ever held meaning to him. More, he had destroyed them.

"Did you see, Doug? The impossible made possible."

Doug had emerged from gate seven, holding a box with several more modified Roombas. "Yes, sir."

"Good. Put in a call. Have someone come and get these extensions. There may be serviceable components left. Let nothing go to waste. Then, follow me. We'll stop at customs next. There are two more Box awaiting me there and three more beyond. I've work still to do."

He walked off without waiting for a reply and wondered if Cooper felt this way, empowered and invincible, in charge of his own destiny.

CHAPTER TWENTY-ONE

Amid the chaos at the passenger terminal, Dyrk was in control and in the zone.

"Game on Titan, game on." His body was tight, tense with anticipation. The world was more focused. It was go-time.

He cracked his neck dramatically.

The action hero rolled out from behind the column Coop had been using as a shield. Dyrk appreciated shields. He understood the utility of them, but he didn't like them. They slowed the action and were, at best, a regrettable necessity.

I didn't realize you had a philosophy about shields.

«Me either.»

Allow me to offer another way to think about them.

«Be my guest.»

The action stops when you're dead.

«Ohhhh...»

Now you get it. Get back to work.

Dyrk launched himself into a roll that brought him behind one of the cops who tried in vain to take on the Box while maintaining his position beyond the range of the fear gun. The man was distracted, his back to Dyrk as he directed ineffective fire at the nearest Doos avatar. Dyrk dealt a single, swift blow to the man's neck, and he crumpled at his feet.

It took only a moment to rifle through the unconscious man's gear and come up with an energy pistol and two backup power packs. After all, it wasn't like they were going to do the cop any good. Dyrk took off and darted to his next position before the police officer's comrades realized Dyrk wasn't quite on their side. He wasn't against them, per se, but he wasn't an ally. Allies didn't leave you unconscious and unarmed.

Dyrk came out from behind cover—a little more carefully this time—and raised the liberated pistol to fire at the Doos. One of the Box had just crossed his line of sight, its back to him as it fixed its attention on the police. Dyrk had a perfect view of its profile.

He set the pistol aside and withdrew his modified stun baton, then rummaged in a pocket until he came up with the enhancer cap he'd taken from the security guard earlier that day. It snapped into place, but he kept the pistol close at hand, just in case. The frequency and modulation of the baton had been precisely set and, when applied to the correct spot, it could incapacitate a Box. Even so, that was no guarantee that the discharge produced by the cap would work, that the modification worked across distance, or even that the Doos extensions had the same design flaw that had let him take out three other avatar configurations earlier in the week. Still, it was worth a shot—literally.

He aimed just above where the Box's hip would have been if it had a more humanoid shape. A bolt of electrical energy shot out of the baton and struck home. The avatar jerked and spasmed, then went still.

Thank god that worked. That makes things a bit easier.

Dyrk didn't reply. He was still in the zone. He didn't have time for distractions or celebration. Heroes didn't stop to congratulate themselves during the action. A teenage girl and an alien...*thingy* needed saving. This was the mission he'd been created for.

Bullets and shrapnel flew around the room, but they didn't touch Dyrk as he stalked through the smoke like an avenging angel.

Didn't we just talk about the benefits of shields and cover?

«Ben?»

Yes?

«Hush. I'm working here.»

If it wasn't so self-defeating, I'd smack the hell out of you when I get my body back.

Dyrk chuckled.

On the far side of the Doos formation, Tycho had rallied. Her eyes didn't show any sign of recognition, but her actions revealed she'd understood the message behind Coop's announcement over the bullhorn.

The young woman had risen like a pale wraith. She had a Doos weapon extended in each hand. Potato clung to her shoulder, its tongue unfurled and tasting the air. Her face showed no emotion. She stepped over a duffel bag and a mangled hard-shell guitar case. Death stalked from the muzzles of her weapons, capturing the nearest Doos before it could retreat. Tycho glanced in its direction and alternated shots from her weapons, blasting the Doos in its tracks. Her shooting was instinctual. The slugs of molten metal weren't as effective at close range, but the momentum of her endless barrage was enough to lift the Box avatar off its treads and send it crashing to the floor. Tycho used the vulnerable moment to close with it, climb onto its torso, and double tap the Box in the chest from close range.

The avatar sputtered and died.

Back near the police, Dyrk continued his whirling-dervish-of-destruction impersonation. He leapt atop the back of a bench, and his toes danced along its rails. Ahead, a Doos turned its attention from the police. It raised a pair of weapon limbs and sighted him.

The Doos fired.

At the same time, Dyrk took another step and jumped straight up. His legs kicked out to the sides in a full split and his hands came together, grasping his pistol in a double-handed grip. He didn't even aim. His weapon barked twice.

By the time Dyrk's feet hit the back of the bench again, the Doos had gone still. Two smoking holes in its carapace stood as testimony to the action hero's shooting prowess. A trickle of smoke also rose from the crotch of Dyrk's pants.

He craned his neck and looked at his trousers. Hesitating a moment, he poked a finger down there and was relieved to find nothing more than a superficial singe along the inseam.

Dyrk. I cannot tell you how lucky you just got. If that...if that had... I can't even say it. Just don't do that again. You won't have to worry about the Box. I'll kill you myself. Are we clear?

Dyrk was mortified. «Yes, sir. It won't happen again.»

See that it doesn't.

Dyrk sighed. More than anything, he wanted to experience all the good stuff humanity had to offer. He knew enough from the endless cutaways and fades-to-black that defined him to know that he needed that piece of anatomy to fully enjoy it.

He jumped off the bench and dropped to his knees. His pistol came up, and he scanned the battlefield for his next target.

Meanwhile, Tycho had emerged from her luggage-fort. She had homed in on another Box. If the arrogant machine intelligence had any understanding of humanity and its propensity for destruction, it would have chosen a different course of action. Instead, it extended its arms like an angry octopus and sped right at the young woman.

Tycho didn't seem to care. Given her mindless rage, she couldn't be concerned about anything. She pulled the trigger on the weapon in her right hand. It clicked, empty. She dropped it where she stood and raised the weapon in her left hand.

The Doos seized the opportunity, perhaps inspired by Tycho's action or maybe thought better of blasting for fear of injuring Potato. It detached one of its limbs and launched it at her. The weapon slammed into Tycho's left hand, shattering her wrist and sending her remaining firearm flying.

Tycho didn't blink. She bent over and extended her hands to the ground.

The Box saw its chance and accelerated.

Tycho stood, wrenching a slab of marble from the battered terminal floor, her delicate hands gripping it tightly.

She charged on her bare feet at the Doos.

The Doos rushed toward her.

Tycho leapt into the air. She extended the hunk of marble over her head and, just before their momentum brought them crashing together, she swung her arms forward and drove the corner of the slab into the avatar's chest, where two pieces of its protective carapace joined.

The sound was incredible, like a thunderclap in the desert. The Doos and Tycho crashed together, then were flung apart by the kinetic force they had unleashed. The girl was somehow holding on to the piece of flooring.

The avatar tipped onto its side but used its arms to arrest its fall. When it had regained an upright state, it turned its sensors to search for the young woman who had taken Potato prisoner.

It found her two feet away, with the marble slab still clutched between her bleeding fingers. The Doos tried to make sense of it.

It never got the chance.

A moment later, the marble slab rested amid the shredded internal workings of the avatar's abdomen, having been driven there by ninety savage pounds of humanity. Tycho paused long enough to acquire new weapons from her opponent's robotic corpse.

When Tycho had struck the Doos with the marble slab, everything and everybody in the terminal had stopped. It was like God had hit the pause button. Combat ceased. The wounded stopped screaming. Everybody stared at the site of the titanic impact.

Except Dyrk.

He used the distraction to maneuver behind the Doos who had been projecting fear at the police. He jammed his modified stun baton into the Box's hindquarters. The machine jerked and slumped forward on its tracks, as he'd hoped it would.

Just like that, the battle resumed.

Not being shot at for a second was nice.

«Was it?»

Dyrk didn't wait for a reply. He was halfway to Tycho, and four Doos were still in action. In front of him, two menaced the girl, and two behind him harassed the cops. No time for chitchat. Plus, the swing in momentum and sudden cessation of the fear gun had allowed the cops to regroup. They advanced. He had to move.

So, that's what Dyrk did. He moved and spun and juked his way across the terminal-cum-arena.

And then he tripped.

He fell right over the prone body of a sleeping alien. Dyrk lay sprawled face-to-face with the xenon. All it did was snore.

Wow, those sleep gas grenades are pretty impressive.

«Ben, I have never noticed you have any trouble sleeping.»

Dyrk pushed up just in time for a bullet to graze his back. He dropped back and rolled to his right three times, and came to a knee with his gun out.

A pair of Box had zeroed in on him. Worse, they knew who he was.

"Give up, Mr. Cooper. You are in violation of your contract."

Oh, you are fucking kidding me!

He pushed his way back into control of his body, sputtering with rage.

"You want to talk violation? Where's my signing bonus? Where's my blockbuster movie deal? Your people didn't enter into that contract in good faith. You want to mess with me about contracts? You've never been taken to task by a Hollywood lawyer. I'm going to tie you up with so many depositions, countersuits, and nuisance litigation that you'll need to manufacture more extensions just to keep track of the paperwork!"

He dropped back, yielding control to Dyrk.

Kick his ass!

Dyrk obliged. He fired, rolled to his left, and fired again. He repeated the maneuver until he managed to put one Box between him and its compatriot.

Nice move! Coop applauded. *One opponent beats two any day of the week.*

«And it looked cool.»

In their mind, Coop cheered.

Dyrk swapped a fresh power pack and shot. He shot again. He unloaded on the Box. It was a lethal barrage, and the alien paid the price, but not before its targeting sensors landed a blow of its own.

A dozen razor-sharp needles blasted into Dyrk's leg, chewing through the flesh an instant before the pain seared through Dyrk's shared brain. He dropped his weapon in shock and grabbed his thigh. Blood seeped between his fingers. He fell to his knees.

«What was that?»

Pain. Welcome to being human. Now stop asking questions and get us out of harm's way.

Dyrk concentrated and directed the virus to repair the leg. He felt the pain and discomfort while it pushed the metal needles from his flesh, regrew the shredded tissue, and reknit the damaged bone. He also knew the remaining Doos was still there.

He looked up and saw the Box had worked its way around to his left. It pivoted, and its treads picked its way through rubble and crushed snoozing bodies littering the terminal's floor. Dyrk reached for his pistol but realized it was on the floor beyond his reach. He pulled out his stun baton and saw the cap had cracked. Things looked bad.

Then Tycho came charging in.

The young woman's face was as blank as a plague mask but with less humanity. Her empty features stood in stark contrast to her violent actions. Tycho fired wildly. She sprinted at the Box. It swiveled to engage her but recoiled when it saw Potato clinging to her shoulder. The brief pause allowed her to get in a hit to Box on its neck.

The avatar's head tilted. Tycho threw her weapon to the floor and jumped like a tiger on top of the Box. Her blood-stained hands grabbed the avatar's shoulders, and her lithe legs wrapped around its torso.

«That hospital gown isn't doing much for her modesty.»

Are you going to tell her that?

«Nope.»

Tycho thrust a hand into the opening in the avatar's neck. She grunted savagely, tearing her hand on something inside it. She yanked with a force that belied her size, but then this was the same girl who'd ripped a hunk of marble from the floor. Her shredded hand pulled free with a tangle of wires and hardware clasped between her fingers as if she had torn out its beating heart. She held her prize up to the sky, an offering to some dark god.

«Let me rephrase that,» Dyrk amended. «Not a chance in Hell.»

Good call.

Dyrk flexed his leg. «Almost there,» he announced for Coop's benefit.

Tycho dropped from her fresh kill and scuttled on all fours to where her last weapon lay. Potato clung on for dear life, but it flashed a tongue-filled grin in Dyrk's direction.

Potato seems happy.

«It lives off pheromones and adrenaline. It's high as a kite right now.»

Like I said. Happy.

Dyrk nodded. Tycho picked up her weapon and jumped on the metallic carcass of the last Doos he'd taken out. The young woman knelt, brought her weapon to her shoulder, and fired back the way she'd come. She sent the last two Box scattering.

Dyrk's leg felt good enough to stand on.

That was quick.

«Yeah, the more I practice, the easier it gets to focus the virus. Just think of all the things we can explore if we don't have to worry about permanent damage. Cool, huh?»

Let's survive this first, and then we'll talk.

Dyrk regained his feet and darted to his left to retrieve his pistol. One of the Box had just gone that way with its attention focused on Tycho. It was a distraction that Dyrk intended to capitalize on.

He had to put on a burst of speed, but he managed to stay out of the line of sight of the avatar's sensors. He shuffled to his left and did his best not to flinch when the police began firing again. Bullets went all over the place.

«Where did these people learn to shoot?» he asked.

If I had to guess, from the movies.

Dyrk ran and ducked behind another support pillar, where he paused and sucked air. He heard the Box coming closer and ventured a look out.

«Perfect.»

The Box trundled right toward him. Backward.

Dyrk stepped out from his hiding place, held his pistol inches from the weak spot Tycho had revealed on the avatar's neck, and fired. The Box never knew what hit it. It just jerked and shut down. Dyrk stepped in casually, using its body as a shield while he peered out at the apocalyptic scene that had been the passenger terminal.

That left just one Box and a couple dozen cops.

And one Tycho.

«I almost feel bad for the Box. She's gonna destroy them.»

Do you? Really?

«No. I don't. Screw Doos.»

That's my boy.

Dyrk maintained his position of cover and watched Tycho.

She took hold of what remained of an arm from one of the fallen Box. With Potato still perched on her shoulder, she charged the remaining avatar and bludgeoned it, striking it over and over with her improvised club.

Doos did its best to fend her off, but she was too close for it to fire on her with any of its limb weapons. It flailed and attempted to restrain her, squeezing her tight with those tentacle-like arms. Their edges cut into her, but she ignored them and continued mindlessly snapping off bits of the avatar with each blow.

Blood flowed from her numerous lacerations. The Box gyrated wildly, trying to avoid Tycho's attack, but it couldn't win. She continued to heal with miraculous speed while Doos didn't heal at all.

Tycho tore a gap in the avatar's chest console. She wedged a hand into the opening, placed her feet on its chest, and heaved against the bolts and fasteners to pry it apart.

The Box pulled one of its limbs free and smashed it across her face. The blow scored a large gash across Tycho's forehead. She froze. Blood flowed into her eyes, blinding her. By the time she pulled a hand free to wipe the blood away, the gash had already healed over.

That is incredible.

«Is that another way to say 'scary?'»

Yes.

The young woman growled and redoubled her efforts. She

wrapped her legs around the avatar's torso and wedged her club into the gap she'd created in its armor. Doos swung at her again, with little effect. Without relinquishing her grip or grasp, she pivoted in place and avoided the worst of its attacks. She moved like a Tasmanian devil that had gotten ahold of some PCP.

Tycho had jammed her makeshift club far enough into the Box to allow her to use it like a lever. She wrenched it savagely, and the carapace tore at one corner.

That was what she'd been waiting for.

The battered teen yanked her weapon free and plunged her bloody arm into the Box's chest.

The Doos tried to seize her. Blood flowed around its weapon limbs as it strove to rip her away.

It succeeded, and Tycho fell to the floor, but she did so clutching a handful of the avatar's internal parts.

It came to an abrupt stop. Tycho didn't move, only lay on her back and panted. After a few breaths, all her cuts had healed enough for the bleeding to stop. All of the Doos extensions had been defeated.

Dyrk turned his head to check on the police. They had rallied and were being organized into a line ten cops across and two deep.

«Ben, I don't see this ending well.»

For who? Tycho or the cops?

«Yes. And for us.»

I suspect you're right. Got any brilliant ideas?

«Also yes, but...»

But Dyrk never finished the sentence. He was distracted by the arrival of two additional Doos avatars. The duo ignored the police, plowing right through their line. They advanced on Tycho where she lay prone on the floor.

It was a fatal mistake.

Tycho's virus had long since restored her. She sat up. Her gown was a wreck and hung in tattered strips from her shoulders, covered with a mélange of blood, dirt, and other stains. Her face bore similar smears, which made the eagerness in her dead eyes more disturbing.

She looked left and right. She stood. Both Box drew closer.

Dyrk stayed still.

There are only two of them left, and they can't afford to let her escape, Coop thought. *So they better be careful.*

«They've been careful not to hurt Potato the whole time. It hasn't worked out well.»

Tycho cracked her neck. She leaned over and placed her hands on the floor before rising with her fists clenched.

She turned to face one of the Doos squarely. It raised its weapons and slowed, but continued forward.

Tycho tilted her head side to side like a curious dog.

She broke into a sprint. She ran right at the Doos, and after five steps, she threw her hands out. A cloud of rocks, bits of ground glass, and dust filled the air in front of her. The avatar's weapons systems sprang to life. It blindly fired its non-lethal rounds, and its companion, which had been tracking Tycho, did the same. She slid to her side, and her speed carried her inside the reach of the second avatar's weapons.

She came to her feet with a blank expression on her face and a fresh slab of concrete clutched in her hands.

«Ben?»

Yes, Dyrk. What is it?

«I don't want to watch this, but I can't stop.»

That may be the most human thing you've ever said.

«Humans are sick.»

You aren't wrong, Dyrk. You aren't wrong.

Tycho struck. She growled and howled and grunted. She smashed her improvised weapon into the Doos. Over and over, she brought it down.

The avatar flailed. It struck back, but its thrashing was, in the end, useless. The teen could not be deterred. She was a machine devoid of emotion and pain. More, Tycho was a weapon incarnate. One extension or ten, Doos never stood a chance.

After what seemed like an eternity, Tycho struck one last blow. She whipped around and placed her back against the mangled avatar's torso. Her right hand reached for one of the weaponized arms. She pulled it to her body and aimed it at the remaining Doos.

Potato rose on its little legs and looked over the top of Tycho's head. It licked her scalp frantically.

The last Box had nowhere to go. It couldn't shoot Tycho, and she had it dead to rights.

The Doos rotated its torso one-hundred and eighty degrees and ran. It didn't get far. Tycho lacked mercy.

She opened fire on the avatar's back. Her weapon bucked four times, and when it stopped, her opponent lay face-down with a massive hole through its body. Its treads still whirred above the marble floor.

Tycho pressed the release on the weapon she held and disconnected it from the dead avatar. She hooked it under her arm and stepped away from its previous owner.

Potato hopped back to her shoulder and resumed licking her neck.

Nearby, a police commander shouted. "They're down. Prepare to advance. We want to take her alive...if we can."

Tycho turned toward the gathered officers. Her eyes swept over them, her head swiveling side to side. It was not an appreciative look. It was a predatory one.

«This is not good. If she can demolish those Doos like that, she's gonna kill those cops.»

I'm afraid you're right. Dyrk, it's time for me to take over.

«Gladly. She's all yours.»

CHAPTER TWENTY-TWO

Coop shook his head and arms. It cleared away the weird sensation that came with resuming control of his own body.

He took a last look at the scene unfolding in the terminal. The cops had regrouped and were preparing to march on Tycho. She looked frighteningly unimpressed.

"All right, Ben Cooper," he whispered to himself. "This is as close to that starring role the Box promised you as you're going to get on Titan. Time to put on a show."

The vibrant and renewed actor—looking and feeling thirty years younger than when he'd arrived earlier in the month—dusted himself off and wet his lips. He licked his hand and ran it through his hair. Twice, to make sure. One could not leave these things to chance.

Coop stepped out from behind the Doos he'd been using as a shield. He rose to his full height, extended his chest and jaw, and just freaking exuded authority.

He walked with confidence toward Tycho. She responded by pivoting in place and aiming her weapon at him.

«You know she might shoot you, right?»

"Not helpful," Coop muttered.

He kept walking.

When he was halfway to Tycho, he extended his hand in the most imperious manner he could muster.

"Stand down, soldier!"

Tycho's head tilted to the side. She swiveled her head and looked at Coop.

She did not lower her weapon.

Coop paused. He forced himself to maintain an aura of calm authority. "I said, stand down. You've defeated the enemy. These are allied forces." He gestured toward the police. "Lower your weapon."

The young woman looked at the weapon. She looked at the police. She looked back at Coop.

"I said, stand down!" He stamped his foot for emphasis.

A long moment passed. The police held their line. Coop held his breath.

Tycho lowered her weapon.

Coop did not miss his mark. He strode right to her and grabbed the liberated weapon limb. He set it down carefully, and when he rose, he hooked his elbow in Tycho's own.

"Soldier, it's time for us to make a tactical withdrawal."

The police took a united step forward. Then another.

Coop shot a look their way. "Stay back. I've got this."

The cops continued their march.

"Oh, hell." Coop reached into his pocket and palmed the grenade of sleeping agent he'd scooped up earlier. "I'm gonna pay for this."

He pulled the grenade's pin and tossed it in front of the police.

Coop did not wait to see how they reacted. He tugged on Tycho's arm. "Come on!"

The pair ran pell-mell toward the outer shell of the terminal. The gas behind them billowed and expanded, briefly concealing them from view.

Coop dodged, veering off from the obvious exit of the

passenger terminal and aiming for a maintenance door. He knew from Dyrk's study of the spaceport's blueprints that beyond that door lay a large supply closet filled with cleaning products, custodial gear, and emergency environmental suits. The last of these was not standard for a maintenance room, but made sense in this case. On the opposite side of the small room lay Coop's actual destination: a small airlock to the moon's surface.

The moment they entered the safety of the airlock, Coop wheeled around and pressed the button to shut the double doors. The doors slammed shut without a sound, sealing them inside. He let go of Tycho. She had allowed herself to be dragged this far, but now she looked on the verge of violence. To be fair, it was a little hard to tell.

Potato, on the other hand, seemed quite content. The little alien pranced on Tycho's shoulder before jumping into Coop's arms.

Coop caught it and shifted the alien to his own shoulder. He ran to the large storage bin mounted on the wall adjacent to the airlock's inner door. Inside were several of the bubble-like environmental suits. He scrambled into one with a minimum of difficulty, though Potato did get a little squished, and Coop had to press one hand against it, pinning the little guy against his chest. Through it all, Tycho glared at him.

«Are you sure this is going to work?»

"Hell, no! There's a better than fifty-fifty chance this will kill her."

«Then why are we doing it?»

"Allow me to explain human police. There is an absolute certainty those cops back there are going to lock up somebody today. They are not going to let Tycho walk away. It's fair to assume that when they attempt to detain her, she's going back to full-on war-machine mode. She'll kill a bunch of them, maybe all of them. If not, it will be because they get lucky and kill her first."

«I don't know. She heals faster than I can. I don't think even a headshot is guaranteed to take her down. She's already a freaking zombie.»

"I'm counting on that healing. Also the zombie thing."

«You are?»

"Yeah. Otherwise, my plan doesn't work. Now, before she realizes what we're doing, I need to blow this damn airlock!"

Coop ran to the far side of the airlock and slammed his palm into the emergency exit button. There was a rapid exchange of gases, and the outer doors opened with a massive clang. The familiar, breathable, oxygen-rich air was gone, replaced by Titan's toxic atmosphere.

Tycho whirled to face Coop with that scary face of hers. Then her body shook. She clutched her throat and tried to cough. Her eyes lifted and focused on him.

"Time to go!" He waved his arm in a "follow me" gesture.

Tycho charged. Coop turned and rushed from the airlock onto the tarmac surrounding the terminal.

The young woman in her tattered hospital gown tried to give chase, but her muscles could no longer get the oxygen they needed. Her body couldn't handle the strain. She staggered and stumbled in pursuit. Coop did not look back. He ran like a college football hero whose life was defined by how fast he could cross the field without being taken down by the other team—or in this case, a teenage zombie war machine. The football, in this instance, was Potato. He didn't notice when, less than fifty yards later, Tycho fell to her knees. Convulsions rocked her body, and her fingernails ripped at her throat before she fell to the ground, unconscious.

Coop stopped running and looked behind him, taking in the scene. "Finally." He turned and headed back to Tycho.

«I thought you said you couldn't kill a zombie.»

"You can't kill them. They're already dead. She's just...mostly dead."

«She looks dead, dead.»

"She'll be fine. We just need a car. Quickly."

«It'll take a miracle.»

Coop picked his head up and scanned the area. He did not have much time. The cops might figure out where he'd gone, and once they did, they'd be after them again. On a normal day, there'd be some traffic, luggage carriers, shuttle inspectors, food service carts, even a security cruiser. Today wasn't normal. The panic inside the terminal had resulted in an evacuation of the immediate area.

"Shit."

Then, distorted by the denser atmosphere, Coop heard the sound of an approaching electric engine. He turned to discover a vehicle driving right toward them. He raised his arms and waved frantically, kneeling over Tycho's body.

The vehicle raced closer, and Coop wondered if it was going to stop in time. He rose to his feet and stepped in front of the girl. "Stop!"

The vehicle screeched to a halt. The driver stared out at him, and Coop stared back.

"What the..."

«...hell is that?» Dyrk finished.

"It's...Tycho?"

Coop would have liked to stand and stare a while in complete confusion, but he didn't have that kind of time. The driver had already begun to don an emergency environmental suit of her own and, a few seconds later, opened her door.

Coop fought off the questions running through his brain and picked up Tycho. He opened the back of the vehicle and settled her on the cushioned bench, then hauled himself into the front seat and closed the door behind him.

The other Tycho flipped a switch, commencing the

atmosphere exchange. Within seconds the green light came on, signifying that what passed for Titanian air had been vented and replaced with the more breathable variety, and that it was safe to remove their suits. Coop rushed to take his off, but the woman beat him.

"Coop, stop staring at me like an idiot. It's me, Jessica."

"What?"

«What?»

"It's a long story. Close your mouth. The Box attacked the hotel again, and the virus kicked into overdrive. It worked! It changed my physiology to match Tycho's. Who, it would appear, you have taken for a walk out here without an environmental suit and killed. Are you insane?"

Coop shook his head. It was a lot to absorb, and he wasn't feeling up to being lectured.

"Dammit, a dozen Box couldn't kill her. Her lungs will heal. Every bit of her will heal. I hope."

The doctor shook her head. "It's not just a matter of healing," she insisted. "Her brain needs oxygen, or did you forget about that little detail?"

"Jess, she's been brain dead for months."

The doctor looked back at the unconscious girl who had been her patient for so long.

"I...She...Okay, fine."

«I don't mean to intrude on this bizarre reunion, but the cops are gonna show up here any time now.»

"Dyrk's right. We need to get out of here before the cops show up. We can figure this out once we're somewhere safe."

Jess nodded and turned back to the steering console. She tapped, and a moment later they were on the move.

CHAPTER TWENTY-THREE

By the time Alhiz'khlo'tam had trekked the length of the spaceport and arrived at the passenger terminal, the flavor of the confusion there had changed. The civilians had fled, except for the small number who required medical attention. Even most of these—the more serious cases—had already been carted off. An overworked team from the spaceport's coroner's office moved among the handful of dead. The bodies, in part or whole, had been mangled by the unforgiving treads of the Box avatars, either before or after being shot, often as not by friendly fire.

Doug trailed behind the xenon, carrying a somewhat depleted box of self-propelled vacuum cleaners and high-temperature explosives. Strung out behind him were his own assistants, men and women also in Al's employ who were loading pushcarts and carrying off the chunks of the six Doos extensions their boss had left in his wake. In time, they would harvest the bounty here at the passenger terminal—once the cops left.

For now, the police were in disarray. It was a miracle none had been killed, though several had been injured and two were maimed. Some moved among the broken or melted avatars, poking at them as if to be sure they would not bestir themselves back to life and resume their attack. Others wandered in a daze, caught up in the aftermath of a terror unlike anything they'd ever imagined. Some few were being debriefed by late arriving superiors desperate to understand the carnage around them or make sense of the repeated insistence that it had all been caused by a teenage hospital patient.

Amid this chaos, sitting in a bubble of calm at a table liberated from one of the sideline shops, were two figures who didn't belong in such a scene. A man and a woman waited, as if for an arriving passenger—not some beloved family member coming to Titan for a joyous reunion, but more like meeting a business associate who had much to answer for. Which, all things considered, was a fair description.

The man was average height, not merely slim but gaunt. He had a florid complexion and dull brown hair to match a pair of unremarkable brown eyes. He wore an impeccable handmade suit, one of a dozen—or so the rumor went—that had each cost more than the price of the shuttle ticket to Milan, where he'd waited while the tailor and his team of apprentices measured, cut, and sewed them. He worried the business end of an unlit cigar like a dog with a bone.

The woman was tall, and where her companion looked thin to the point of ill health, she was slender and lithe. She was as pale as the dress of silk and polar bear fur that covered her from shoulder to ankle. Her eyes revealed a blue so milky they hinted she might be blind. Her hair fell like a satin waterfall of darkness down her back, ending at mid-thigh. Her only nod to coloration were her lips, painted a flaming red.

Al walked to their table. In its way, it was a remarkable meeting. The three of them never met together in the flesh. He gave a curt nod, settled into a chair facing them so he wouldn't loom, and acknowledged them by name.

"Diamond Queen. Big Tony."

"Alhiz'khlo'tam," replied the woman. Her voice was little more than a breath. Big Tony offered nothing. He returned the nod and chomped on his cigar.

"What brings you out, together, on this fine day?"

"Don't get cute," snapped Big Tony. "You're in violation of our agreement."

"How so?"

"This. All a this." The crime boss gestured around them, pointing with his cigar. "It's bad for business."

"I agree, but I fail to see how I'm responsible for it."

"We acknowledge that the Box represent an implacable and invincible species," stated the woman. "One that needs must be endured at times. Still, under the terms of our agreement, you are responsible for all xenons on this station. Accountability for current events falls to you."

"Not to be too technical, but the Box here are not xenons. They are the remote avatars of a machine intelligence located lightyears away."

Big Tony bristled. "Are you back to being cute?"

"Not at all," replied Al, his own voice calm and soothing without a hint of subservience. "I merely point out the realities of the situation. It is a difficult thing to impose order on a being who is not present. One cannot apply influence upon, let alone control, such an individual."

"And yet," breathed the Diamond Queen, "as has been noted, their actions do not serve our respective business interests. What are you doing to remedy this circumstance?"

"I've destroyed them."

Another gesture with a cigar took in the shattered and mangled Box extensions. "No, that's what some mutant kid did, least as far as we've heard so far."

"Only these," responded Al, and his eyes seemed to gleam. His lips curved up into a slight smile. "On my way here, I personally ended six others."

"Are you overstating your case?" asked the Diamond Queen.

"We are aware of your history, how and why you came to be here on Titan. No one—with maybe the exception of whatever mutant child the police allowed to escape—can take out Doos, let alone six of it. You know that to be impossible, better than any of us."

Big Tony grunted in agreement.

Al's smile broadened. "It is fair to say that I have had a change of perspective. There are no longer any extensions of Doos on Titan. Should any more arrive, you have my word I will handle them myself, without delay and with great prejudice."

"That is…satisfactory," replied the Diamond Queen. She stood and walked away, acquiring a security escort that seemed to appear from nowhere.

"And you, Big Tony, are you satisfied?"

The crime boss stood. He removed his cigar and shrugged. "I'm good, but see, there's one more piece."

"A piece?"

"Your Doos, one of it had a…let's call it a deadman transmitter. It sent a signal to every bounty hunter on Titan. There's a sizable retrieval fee on offer for anyone who recovers that doctor the previous Box had out at their ranch, dead or alive. My sources tell me you've been hosting her in your fancy hotel, so I'm assuming you're connected, given your past history with Doos. Also, there's a still bigger bounty for the safe return of some alien critter of the Box what got stolen."

Al's grin turned to a frown. "Per the terms of our agreement, supervision of retrievers is under your domain. Can you call them off?"

"I already did so, soon as that signal went out. Seemed prudent, until I checked in with you, the bounty being provided by a xenon and all."

"I appreciate that."

"There's just one problem. Several of them, the bounty hunters, have not fired back an acknowledgment. Might be legit comm problems, might be they're just ignoring the call so they can pursue the reward now and whine plausible deniability later."

"Meaning what, exactly?"

Big Tony put his cigar back between his teeth. "Meaning, there're a couple teams still out there looking to make their score by taking out that doctor of yours."

CHAPTER TWENTY-FOUR

Jessica took several quick turns and managed to get them from the terminal and into what amounted to traffic on Titan. She needed to think.

Potato needed attention or something. It wouldn't sit still. Instead, it bounded around the cabin. First it stood in Coop's lap and licked his face. Then it ran over to Jessica and did the same until she tossed it back to Coop so she could concentrate and drive.

Finally, Potato hopped to the back of the vehicle and went to Tycho. It positioned itself next to her head and began to nuzzle and lick the young woman's face.

"What's with Potato?" Coop asked.

"I have no idea. Well, no, I do have an idea, but I don't have enough information. I know where we can get it, though. Hold on."

Jessica's fingers danced on the control console and keyed in Al's comm code. A moment later, the alien's face appeared on the windshield in front of her.

"Dr. Acorns. Cooper. You've been busy this morning. The passenger terminal is a mess, and the police are more than a little distraught. My...business associates have taken me to task for these events, and I am attempting to tie up some loose ends even as we speak. More on that in a moment. How may I help you?"

Coop looked at her. "He knows about your transformation?"

She shrugged and focused on the call. "Al, I have some questions."

"As do I." The alien sighed.

"Was that all of the Box extensions? Did Mr. Cooper get them all, or are there still more running around looking for us?"

Al nodded. "Yes. The avatars at the terminal were the last remaining Doos extensions on Titan."

Coop chewed his lower lip. "Are you sure? I wasn't keeping too close a count, but I don't think there were enough back there to cover all of them."

"You are quite astute, Cooper. I was inspired by your actions today and eliminated a few myself. I assure you, all twenty of Doos' avatars have been accounted for."

"That's a relief," Jessica replied. "Okay, next question. Have your people taken all of the medical equipment out of Scatola's habitat at the Box ranch yet?"

"No, it made more sense to sort and inventory it all in place. It wasn't, shall we say, a priority. I had them set up a security perimeter to keep it secure until after you were on your way. My people and I have been kept quite busy trying to arrange for your needs and covering your human butts from everyone who wants to hurt you. It's been a full-time job. Besides, I am still working to line up the right buyers. Doing so takes time, which has been in short supply since I met you. Why?"

"Because I need more data, and I need some of those machines to get it."

Al nodded. "Now for my questions. When and why did your patient wake up? And why did she decide to go to the terminal and take on a small army of Box judges? Most important, how in the universe did she defeat them?"

Jessica looked uncomfortable. "Al, those are just a few of the questions I need that equipment to answer."

The alien sighed again. "Very well. You are welcome to it, but… Dr. Acorns, I expect you to share those answers with me. Are we agreed?"

"We are." She killed the connection before the xenon could change his mind or make other demands. Jessica turned her face toward Coop. "That's as close to good news as we could get for the moment."

Cooper looked back at her. "That's good, because Dyrk says we're being followed."

Jessica gasped. "What do you mean we're being followed?"

Coop rolled his eyes. "Uh…I thought it was self-explanatory. Now listen, honey—"

"Don't call me that. How many times do I have to say it?"

He shrugged. "If you can hold off on lecturing me about my rampant chauvinism, I'd like you to concentrate on the people following us."

She gripped the wheel more tightly. "Sorry. Where are they?"

"Dyrk said they're three vehicles back. Make a turn and see if they stay with us."

Jessica took a left around a large warehouse, and sure enough, a small transport with two occupants made the turn with them.

"Okay, what do I do?" she asked.

"You stay calm and keep driving."

"Should I head for the ranch?"

"No. Not until we shake them."

"How are we going to do that?"

"Good question."

When Jessica looked back, she saw that the transport had pulled closer. "He's coming up on us."

The other vehicle increased its speed still more and pulled alongside them. Two occupants—one human and one short pinkish alien—waved at them to follow their vehicle.

Coop shook his head and waved them off.

The men brandished weapons and waved back. The human had a shit-eating grin on his face.

Jessica's heart went cold. Sweat beaded on her back and her heart rate increased. Her knuckles grew white on the controls.

"Jess, time to shake these guys."

Jessica stared straight ahead. She tried to get her breathing under control.

Coop wouldn't shut up. "Jess? I said it's time to shake these guys. Are you okay?"

The doctor shook her head. "No. I am not okay. I'm trying to be. Be quiet for a second. I need to concentrate."

She slowed her breathing. She took in deep breaths and flexed her fingers. It felt better.

She slammed the accelerator forward, and their transport raced from the other vehicle.

"Whoa! Go, Jess." Coop laughed.

"It's just logic. They can't shoot at us if they can't open their doors. Since they didn't have environmental suits on, we're safe from that threat for now."

"Oh, yeah. That does make sense."

"Of course, it does. I'm a scientist, Mr. Cooper."

"Right. Now, science us out of this mess and ditch these guys so we can get to the ranch."

Jessica opened her mouth to reply but shut it when the other vehicle sped up and rammed them from behind.

"Oh no," she mouthed before she made a quick left turn and created some distance.

"Don't 'oh no' me. Lose them. Ram them back. Do something!"

"Right. Right…"

Jessica put the car through another series of turns. She weaved around larger cargo transports that flowed between the area's warehouses, using them to block their pursuers. Coop turned in his seat. "They're coming up fast on the left."

She nodded and cut right, skating across the path of another vehicle, avoiding being T-boned, then slowed to match its pace, lost from the sight of her pursuers.

Their would-be assailants got caught with the vehicle between. They waved their weapons at the unsuspecting driver and mouthed obscenities through the glass. It didn't matter. She had the distraction she'd wanted and used it, making a quick right turn, losing the thugs. She sped off perpendicular to them.

"Nice move, Jess!"

"I know."

She made another right and accelerated along the road. Seconds ticked by, and Jessica made a wide circuit of the warehouse sector.

After a few minutes, Coop faced forward again. "All clear. We lost them."

She sighed in relief and looked at the navigation panel. She needed to make the next left. They had to sweep around the outskirts of the terminal and get on the road to the former Box habitat.

Jessica rotated the controls and moved into the flow of traffic on the ring road. "Is Tycho okay?"

Coop turned in his seat. Tycho looked as fine as Tycho always looked. "I don't think she noticed anything."

"Okay. Who were those guys?"

"I don't know."

Her heart rate began to slow back to normal. She glanced at the comms console and realized it had been flashing since that other vehicle had begun following them. Jessica looked at the incoming code. "It's Al." She tapped the button to open the chat.

"Dr. Acorns. You disconnected before I could share some vital information."

"Did it have something to do with thugs trying to ram us off the road?"

Al shrugged. "It might. Prior to the demise of the last Doos, it appears to have issued a bounty for the lot of you. My associate has final say over all bounty hunters on Titan and has sent a message to call them off, but a few may have gone rogue. They are still looking for you. As are the police."

"I appreciate the heads up, but it's a bit late."

"Something perhaps for you to remember the next time you think to terminate a call."

Coop shook his head. "This just keeps getting better and better."

The alien's onyx head bobbed in an exaggerated imitation of a human nod. "Are you near the habitat?"

"We're about to make the turn that leads in that direction. We should be there in…ack!"

Jessica shrieked. A different vehicle sideswiped her side of the transport. A leering face laughed at her and pointed a gun her way. Her hands flew to her face and covered her eyes.

«Ben, steer this thing!»

Coop grabbed for the wheel and spun them away from the new attacker.

"Dr. Acorns, are you all right?" Al's calm settled her panic before it could begin.

"Sorry!" she replied and lowered her hands back to the controls, shoving Coop's hand away. "I am so sick of these bastards! I am sick of people trying to kill me!" She jerked the controls to the left and slammed into the other vehicle, then peeled off.

"I am sick of aliens and criminals trying to kill my friends!" She accelerated and slammed into her attackers again. "No offense, Al. You've been lovely."

"None taken."

"I just want to do my work and be safe and healthy! Leave. Me. Alone!"

Jessica braked, falling behind the other vehicle, then she accelerated again and slammed into it from the rear. She shoved against the jackasses who had attacked them and watched with satisfaction as the driver struggled to regain control.

«This is a new side of the good doctor. Who knew she was such a badass?»

Coop looked over at her, grinning broadly. "What do we say to the thugs?"

"Not today."

She slammed the accelerator to the floor, pushing her victims ahead of her until the vehicle slid sideways and spun out into oncoming traffic. Jessica turned in her seat and watched. A massive cargo hauler smashed into the little vehicle, flipping it end over end.

When it tumbled to a stop, its doors were wide open.

"You won't be getting any trouble from them," Al mused.

Coop looked over at Jess, who was breathing heavily. "Are you okay?"

She nodded. "Yeah. I am. That felt...good."

Al chuckled. "I can see you will be just fine. I will meet you at the Box habitat as soon as I can get free. I have a few final tasks to deal with here."

The comm closed, and Jessica stared out her windshield. She smiled the entire way to the ranch.

CHAPTER TWENTY-FIVE

Jess parked the vehicle in the garage that had been Scatola's research habitat only the week before, one of three such complexes that comprised the previous Box team's ranch. Once the atmosphere was good, she jumped out and ran inside to prep the equipment or something like that. Coop didn't ask many questions. He just walked to the rear of the vehicle and opened the hatch.

Tycho looked horrible. She didn't have any open wounds, but her body was covered in dried blood, dirt kicked up from Titan's surface, and who knew what else. Her petite chest rose and fell with the even, gentle breaths of deep, restful sleep.

"She looks so peaceful," offered Coop.

«For now. If she wakes up, who knows what she'll do. Let's hurry.»

"Good idea."

Coop cradled Tycho in his arms and carried her into the habitat and down the main corridor to the laboratory.

Jess was busy powering up equipment. "Just put her on the table," the doctor called over her shoulder.

"Should I strap her down?" Coop asked.

"What do you think?"

"Right. War movies."

Coop did as Jess instructed. When he finished, he regarded his handiwork. Tycho was restrained at the wrists and ankles with flexible polymer bands that were stronger than steel. Another pair of straps pinned her at the chest and pelvis.

"Think that'll hold her?"

«Every movie I've ever seen says 'no.'»

Coop placed his finger on his chin and considered this. Like Dyrk, he'd seen a lot of movies.

"You're totally right."

He rummaged through the cupboards and made a trip to the supply room. Ten minutes later, he stood over Tycho and again surveyed the results of his efforts.

"She looks like the victim of a bad bondage porno."

«I've never seen one of those.»

"You have no idea how relieved I am to hear that."

Satisfied, Coop stepped back and almost tripped over Potato. The little guy had pressed against the side of the examination table and was trying to scale it. When he'd stuffed the weird creature into his environmental suit before luring Tycho out of the airlock, it had been purple, its skin still exposed from being shaved. Now that flesh lay hidden by a blue-green striped fuzz.

"When did you grow that, buddy? Just now, while we were in the car?"

Potato's little legs kept scrambling against the table but couldn't get any purchase. Even if they had, physics was not in its chubby favor.

Coop bent over and took Potato into his arms and stroked its back. The new fur was so short it bristled.

"What's up with you, little buddy?" he wondered aloud.

«I think it's trying to get to Tycho.»

Sure enough, Potato squirmed and pumped its legs until

finally Coop set it on the table. The alien ran up Tycho's body to her neck and nestled in next to her face. It calmed right away.

Moments later, Jessica returned. She saw Potato and picked it up.

Upon being hefted from its nest against Tycho, it emitted a horrible squeal of protest. It was a terrible, keening sound that set Coop's hair on end. Jess dropped it in shock, and Potato seized the opportunity to return to its position in the crook of the teen's neck.

"I didn't know it could make noise," Coop remarked.

Jess paused and considered it. "Potato has all the necessary anatomical equipment, but your assumption wasn't a bad one. In all my time with it, it's never once vocalized anything like that. This is very interesting."

"I just thought it was annoying."

"You aren't wrong about that either." Jess shook her head to clear it. "Whatever. You see how its fur is growing back? Things are happening. I need to get these tests running. Who knows how much time we have left." She exited the laboratory.

Coop found a rolling chair and settled into it. He kicked his feet up on the end of Tycho's examination table, leaned back, and tried to relax.

It had been a long day. He needed to close his eyes for a minute, but he had no intention of sleeping, not even a catnap. He just wanted to rest his eyes for a few seconds.

He never got the chance. In the next instant, Tycho gasped with regained consciousness.

Coop's feet fell to the floor. He moved to the girl's side and stared at her. Her back was arched against the numerous restraints, and her breath croaked from her lips.

Potato had leapt from the table and was running rings around Coop's left ankle, but all of Coop's attention was on Tycho.

"Please don't kill me," he mumbled.

«That was just pathetic.»

"Do you not recall how many Box she killed?"

«A fair point. Hey, turns out you were right back at the spaceport. Taking her out onto the surface didn't kill her.»

Coop paid Dyrk no mind. He was too focused on Tycho, who struggled against all her restraints until her body sucked in a huge gout of air, and her eyes flew open. They darted about and finally locked on Coop.

"That's new," he noted.

«I'm learning that new is not always good.»

Tycho's eyes bulged. "Wh…Wh…Wh…?"

Jess entered the lab and froze, one hand holding her tablet and the other raised to point at Tycho. "How is she talking? Her speech centers were blown out ages ago."

Tycho's gaze turned to Jess. The two women locked eyes, and Tycho began to whimper.

«You know, I'd freak out too if I was strapped to a table and my doppelgänger walked in. Just sayin'.»

Jess dashed around the table and grabbed a scanner. She lowered it to the young woman's head and made soothing sounds.

«Ben, is there anything someone could say that would make you feel better in her situation?»

"Nope. I got nothing."

A minute passed. Tycho's eyes continued to dart between Coop and Jess. Her breathing bordered on hyperventilation. Coop grew more nervous by the second.

"Jess…"

She raised a hand to silence him. "One second. This is…amazing."

"What is?"

Jess removed the scanner and smiled. "Her brain is. It's healed. Areas that have been dead or dormant for months are all showing normal levels of activity. It's inconceivable."

Coop looked at Tycho, who clearly understood everything being said, though none of it had an effect on her panic. "Inconceivable? I do not think this word means what you think it means."

CHAPTER TWENTY-SIX

Jess had a bedside manner that left something to be desired, so while the doctor puttered about setting up more tests, Coop pulled his chair closer and sat alongside Tycho. The young woman hadn't uttered another word, but her saucer-sized eyes told him she was terrified.

He took her hand and put on his compassionate face. "Tycho, my name is Ben Cooper. You might recognize me from my movies."

Tycho's expression didn't change.

«I guess she's not a fan.»

Coop grunted. "Honey, you've been through a lot. You were in a coma, but you're okay now. This lady," he jerked a thumb toward Jess, "she's a doctor, and she's going to help you. Heck, she's been helping you. Just stay calm."

«If she doesn't stay calm, it's going to be bad.»

I know. That's why I'm trying to soothe her, Coop thought back.

«Do you think she's still a war machine?»

How would I know? And I'm not going to ask Jess while Tycho can hear us. I think she's going to have enough to adjust to without being told she's been brainwashed and turned into death incarnate.

«That seems wise.»

Gee, thanks. Now, make yourself useful and tell me if she has a thingy like you inside her brain. It seems like something we might like to know.

«Will do. Just keep holding her hand. The connection makes it easier.»

Dyrk faded from Coop's awareness, acting on his request. The actor kept his face calm and friendly, his smile warm without being creepy, and waited. He had no idea how long it took for one artificial, virus-spawned identity to look for another. He wondered if Dyrk even had a clue how to go about it. Minutes later, he felt Dyrk return.

Well?

«Nada. Zip. Zero. I didn't find any trace of another viral echo. I think she's in the clear on that front.»

Okay. What's her virus doing?

«Her virus is active. Crazy active. Aside from the intensity, it doesn't seem to be any different from what we've encountered in you and Jess. Other than me, I mean.»

Coop paused to consider this news. He wanted to tell Jess what Dyrk had learned but didn't think it wise to drop all that info on Tycho. Besides, Potato had been pawing at Coop's foot, desperate to get his attention.

"What's up, little guy?"

In response to Coop's acknowledgment, Potato darted away and pushed its body against Jessica's calf.

The doctor paused. "What is it doing?"

"I think it's trying to herd us together."

"It's adorable, but I have work to do. Please keep it corralled."

Coop rolled his eyes. "Come here, Lassie, er, Potato."

The alien complied, with obvious reluctance. When Potato came within range, Coop scooped it up and scratched its back.

Tycho stared at Potato in shock.

"What is that?" she asked in a hoarse whisper.

Coop looked at her in pleased surprise. "Oh good, you can talk. Um, this is Potato. He's an alien. He's really important to us right now, but that is a long story. Would you like some water?"

Tycho nodded weakly. She stared at Potato while Coop procured a cup of water. He held it to her lips and helped her take a few swallows before setting the cup on a nearby table.

"Is that better?"

"Yes, thank you. What did you say your name was?"

"Ben Cooper, but just call me Coop."

"Okay. Where am I?"

Coop debated how to answer this. In the end, he decided on an honest but safe answer. "You're in a doctor's office on Titan."

"The moon?"

"Yep."

"How did I get here?"

Coop sidestepped that one. "You were brought here and given an experimental treatment. Nothing else had worked for you until Dr. Acorns, Jessica, treated you."

Tycho nodded. "I don't remember any of that."

"Sweetheart, I'm an actor. I don't know much about medicine, but I think that sounds normal for someone who just came out of a coma. I wouldn't sweat it too much."

"No offense, Mr. Cooper..."

"Coop, please."

"Coop, the lady you called Dr. Acorns looks like my identical twin. I'm strapped to this table, and you say I'm on a moon halfway across the solar system. Given all of that, tell me how I'm supposed to take it easy."

"When you say it like that, it sounds a little crazy."

"Yeah. Mr. Cooper, crazy's a good word for it. May I have a blanket? It's cold in here."

Coop stood. "Sorry about that. Let me get you untied first. Then I'll get you that blanket."

«Are you sure it's a good idea to untie her?»

Not totally, but I'm pretty sure.

«We've had worse odds.»

Coop nodded in silent agreement. Then he untied all of Tycho's restraints and draped a blanket around her.

"Thank you," she murmured.

Jess stopped messing with her machines and sat in front of the young woman. Potato climbed up her leg, onto her lap, then jumped onto the examination table and pressed itself against Tycho's hip.

"There is a lot of this you won't understand," the doctor began. "But I don't have time to cover everything. As Mr. Cooper mentioned, you suffered a traumatic brain injury that left you in a coma back on Earth. You were brought here to take part in an experiment. It involved injecting you with an alien virus."

"A virus?" Tycho looked unsettled.

"Yes. It healed you. Physically. It may help you to know that both Mr. Cooper and I also received this virus."

Tycho reached for her cup of water, swallowed the rest of it, and held it out for a refill, which Coop provided.

"Thank you. Oddly, it does."

"One thing about this virus is it's multifaceted, and portions of its process involve a bio-chemical reaction that requires Potato, here. His pheromones act as a catalyst that returns your body to a genetically idealized state. In my case, because my disease was genetic, that meant an idealized state for my disease. So instead of curing me, the virus brought me closer to death. As a final effort to save me, we used your DNA to create a new physical map for my virus to model. Consequently…"

"You look like me," Tycho finished. "I did well in biology class, but this is a lot to take in."

"I know it is."

Everyone got quiet. Except Potato. It seemed thrilled that everyone was in such close proximity and showed it by dancing around in circles alongside Tycho.

The young woman looked at the hyperactive alien. "What is that exactly? I mean, other than a trigger for this virus?"

Coop jumped in. "That's Potato. It's an immortal alien that used to belong to a race of alien jerks called the Box. We don't know all the details about that, and no big loss. What is important is that Jess developed the virus from it."

"Does it always act like this?"

Potato spun in counterclockwise circles. Faster and faster.

"No," Coop and Jess answered in unison.

"It looks happy. Just weird." Tycho reached out to pet Potato. Then things got strange.

CHAPTER TWENTY-SEVEN

Potato stopped spinning and dropped to its belly on the table. Its little eyes darted about and its tongue lolled from its mouth.

Tycho pointed at Potato's back. "What are those?"

Jessica and Coop leaned in for a better look and discovered three small lumps had grown under its short layer of replacement fur. The lumps were moving.

Coop stood back up. "I have no idea, but it's icky."

Jess inched her face closer.

The lumps writhed and grew. They'd started out no bigger than blueberries, but as the seconds ticked by, they increased to the size of golf balls. They were too big to be called lumps anymore. Potato's new fur fell away from the trio of pustules, revealing its lavender skin, stretching as something squirmed with the growths just beneath their surface.

None of it bothered Potato. It seemed beyond content. It didn't move. It just sat there looking happy and stupid until the movement inside the lumps slowed and then stopped entirely. That's when Potato began to keen.

Tycho pulled her toes from the puddle of drool that Potato was depositing on the table. "Yuck."

Potato arched its back, and the keening increased in volume. The pustules throbbed and resumed their growth, this time in rhythm to the throbbing. Potato didn't seem to be crying out in pain, but the noise hurt everyone else in the room. The ululation was high-pitched and just plain awful.

"This sucks," Coop complained.

«Could you cover our ears, please?»

Cooper complied. It helped, but not much.

Potato began rocking back and forth, its first deliberate movement since the now fist-sized protrusions had appeared. As it moved, the pustules swayed, stretching its skin still further as they waggled about.

Jess looked fascinated. Coop tried to keep from throwing up.

With a slow sucking sound, one of the growths dropped to the table with a 'plop.'

Coop shivered. "Eww. That is not okay."

Jessica continued to stare. "Don't be such a baby. This is fascinating."

The second pustule fell and rolled to a stop near the edge of the table. The third followed suit.

Tycho curled into a ball with a look of utter revulsion on her face. Coop knew how she felt.

Silence reigned. Potato stopped moving and settled back onto its belly. Its keening stopped, and once again it was a motionless, short-haired, blue and green lump.

But the lavender pustules moved.

Coop stood on his tiptoes and pointed. "Whoa! Now what's it doing?"

Even Jessica looked shocked. "I don't know." She examined it more closely.

Its eyes popped open and examined her right back.

Jess screeched and fell backward out of her chair.

Coop laughed. "Didn't you just call me a baby?"

The doctor picked herself up. She ignored Cooper and

approached the table where all three growths had now sprouted tiny legs, eyes, and little slits for mouths. They already dangled their tongues onto the surface of the table.

Coop came back to the table and leaned down next to Jess. Even Tycho loosened up enough to peer at the trio of adorable mini-Potatoes. Each of them tottered to one of the nearby humans and insisted on being picked up. They all obliged with varying degrees of enthusiasm. The tiny aliens settled in and began licking.

"Incredible," Jess murmured, her eyes wide with fascination. "Do you know what this means? Do you understand the scientific significance of this, Mr. Cooper?"

"I understand that tater-tots are ruined for me. Forever. That's a crime against humanity."

Jess sighed, but Tycho chuckled.

«Nice one.»

CHAPTER TWENTY-EIGHT

After the shock of the weird alien birth wore off—or they'd all numbed to it—Jess managed to catch Tycho up on everything else that had transpired. All things considered, she took it well. She only had one question.

"How long has it been since I had real food?"

Jess considered. "Many months."

Tycho smiled. "That's what it feels like. Do you have anything to eat?"

"Oh my gosh, of course, but you'll have to go slow. Okay?"

"Sure."

The group adjourned to the kitchen where Dyrk, after speed-reading through several cookbooks they had found in the habitat's digital library, scrounged enough bits and pieces from dry storage to whip up a poor man's frittata.

«Humble beginnings, working with powdered eggs, but I'm already seeing the allure. There's room for so much...creativity.»

"Just don't poison us, okay? And don't take it badly if Tycho doesn't like what you made. She hasn't used her taste buds in a long time."

They ate a wordless meal, punctuated by the occasional

nummy sound, each alone with their thoughts and their miniature alien fuzzballs.

When the dishes were cleared and Coop returned to the table, Jess spoke.

"This changes everything. Absolutely everything."

"Everything? What are you including in everything? And why? Um, not why about what you include, why does it change things?" Coop asked, already nervous.

"I believe we should…no, I believe we *must* stay here on Titan. There is too much to be learned. I need to study Tycho. I need to study all the Potatoes. Not to mention the virus itself. Now I can experiment with it along with Potato's pheromones. This has to be documented, and if we wait, things might change. Earth itself might affect the outcome of the experiments."

"Whoa. Whoa. Can we just slow down a second? We have been risking our lives to get back to Earth. We have an alien crime boss making those arrangements. Again. Let's not forget that the Box may return to Titan looking for us. You know they won't stop until they get Potato back."

Jess nodded. "I know. I know. It sounds crazy to me too, but it feels…right. The potential here is enormous. For science. For medicine. For…humanity." She pointed to Tycho. "This girl was brain dead, and now she's walking around fine. You were days away from dying of cirrhosis, and not only do you now have a healthy new liver, you're thirty years younger! Imagine being able to bring that to the world."

Cooper sighed and put his face in his hands. "It's getting late," he mumbled. "Can we agree to table this until after we get some sleep? I'm exhausted."

"I can agree to that. It's a good idea."

"Okay." Coop stood from the table and went in search of a place to curl up and catch some sleep.

On his way out the door, he heard Tycho whisper to Jess. "He's really thirty years older? Ewww."

CHAPTER TWENTY-NINE

A few hours after the lunch service, but before they opened for dinner, Al sat at his private table in the back of the restaurant at *Palais Titan*. The maître d'hôtel escorted the Diamond Queen and Big Tony his way, and he rose to meet them. Both were dressed to the nines. It had been some time since either had visited the moon's most expensive dining establishment, let alone been Al's guest.

"I've asked the chef to prepare something special for you," explained Al. "I'm confident you'll find it to your liking. First, though, there's a topic I'd like to discuss."

The wine steward appeared at Al's elbow, offering a bottle of champagne for his inspection. Once Al approved, the steward poured three glasses and vanished.

"Are you trying to butter us up before hitting us with this topic of yours?" Big Tony set aside the cigar he'd been chewing and swirled his glass before tossing half of it back.

"Nothing of the kind," assured Al.

"What is the topic?" asked the Diamond Queen.

"Art."

"Art?"

"Allow me to explain."

"Please." She took a sip of her drink, smiled, and took another.

"Recently, I had an epiphany—"

"*Gesundheit*," muttered Big Tony.

Al glared at him. "This will go much faster if you keep the droll comments to yourself and avoid further interruptions."

"Fine. An epiphany."

"That epiphany, which upended things I have believed to be absolute truth for many years, led me to consider other things I imagine we all take for granted."

"Such as?"

"The people of Titan lack hope. Many of them arrive with dreams and ambitions, but all too soon, the reality of this place beats them down. Indeed, the ease with which we three run everything here is due, I now see, to the hopelessness of the residents."

"Is there a point to this?" asked Big Tony. He pointed at the bottle in the champagne bucket.

Al refilled glasses all around the table. The Diamond Queen lifted hers in a brief toast. Big Tony drained his and waggled the glass for another refill before Al had set the bottle down.

"My point is that I believe we can improve the lives of the people here—and by extension improve our respective profits—by establishing a few modest programs in support of the arts."

The Diamond Queen smiled. "And you'd like us to share in the costs?"

Al shrugged. "That's up to you. An investment now would entitle you to a proportional percentage of the profits. I'm prepared to shoulder the burden myself, but if so, I'd prefer to avoid complaints from either of you later that you didn't have the opportunity to get in at the beginning."

Big Tony scowled. "When you say art, are you talking like paintings? You want to open some kind of museum?"

"Painting, yes. I thought we might start with a gallery. Also an institute, modest at first, but with every intention of expanding to include sculpture, literature, music, and theater."

"Does this have anything to do with the recent visit from Doos?" The Diamond Queen's tone was surprisingly soft.

"Indirectly. It is fair to say that the Box would be bewildered by the idea. They don't comprehend art."

"And how is this good for business?"

"It will attract interest. A market where we control the supply, which in turn will drive demand. Art produced on Titan will be sought after precisely because it is unlike anything available anywhere else. Our citizenry will feel they are a part of that."

Big Tony shook his head. "I don't see how that follows."

Al smiled. "It is like the affinity ordinary people back on Earth feel for their local sportsball teams. They do not themselves participate, nor train, nor partake of the extravagant salaries some individuals command. Nonetheless, they become psychologically connected and feel a part of something bigger than themselves. This distracts them from their drab and sorrowful lives."

The Diamond Queen tapped a finger against her champagne glass. "And you believe you can produce a similar effect through art?"

"I just ask you to consider it. What is the Terran expression... sleep on it? Ah, but our dinner comes. Enough of business. Speaking of art, the chef here at the *Palais* creates masterpieces..."

CHAPTER THIRTY

Morning came, and Coop made coffee in the kitchen at the habitat. Jess and Tycho must have been exhausted, so he decided to let them sleep. He settled into a chair with his cup and some instant oatmeal he'd found in a cupboard. His new miniature Potato had snuggled itself on his left shoulder.

«You know, steel-cut oats would taste so much better.»

"How long would that take?"

«Maybe twenty or thirty minutes.»

"This took two. I'm hungry now. Also, we don't have the right supplies."

«Sure, but I'm just saying, next time. Okay?»

"Tell you what. You make a list of ingredients for the things you want to cook—a modest list, don't get crazy on me—and the next time we go to the spaceport, we'll go shopping."

«Deal!»

Coop added some sugar to his coffee and turned on his tablet. He had a message waiting for him. From Al.

Call me

«He doesn't waste a lot of words, does he?»

"No, he does not. I don't know if I should respect that or be terrified."

«Are they mutually exclusive?»

"Not at all. Good point."

Coop tapped the button to reply, triggering the tablet's comm function. The alien answered almost immediately.

"Ah, Cooper. Good morning."

"Good morning, Al. I hope I didn't wake you."

"Small chance of that, Cooper. Clusterans sleep very little compared to humans."

"Good to know. How are things?"

"Things are going well. Your three friends managed to depart the spaceport on the first shuttle this morning. They have arrived at the orbital terminal and should continue on to Earth shortly."

"That is good news." Coop was relieved.

"It is. However, you should know that another Doos avatar arrived soon after."

"That is not good news."

Al shrugged. "It may be. The Box went straight to spaceport security and demanded access to their video feeds. The security folks had been advised to comply in order to keep the Box peaceful and get it back off the moon as quickly as possible. My sources tell me Doos confirmed that three humans with the appropriate identification departed on the shuttle."

"So, Doos bought it?"

"It appears so. After watching the video and checking the manifests, the Doos returned to its own ship and requested an immediate departure slot. It returned to orbit right before I messaged you."

"So, it's gone?"

"It is in the process. The Box ship has changed the original itinerary it had filed. It is now bound for Earth in the next available jump window."

"Doos just doesn't give up, doos it?"

«Heh. Good one, Ben.»

"It would appear not."

Coop considered this news.

"Al, are you certain that if more Box arrive here, you'll know it?"

"I am. I track all arrivals and departures in this section of space. In my experience, the Box are anything but subtle. It would never occur to any of them to be anything less than brazen and overt when they travel, nor can they avoid customs if they wish to enter the spaceport. As a man in the import-export business, I have sources in that line of work."

Coop chuckled. "Okay, thanks for the heads up. I need to talk to Jess about our next move. We'll get back to you."

Al nodded and closed the connection without another word.

«So, what is our next step?» Dyrk asked.

"I don't know. I thought I'd be pumped to return to Earth. Now, I'm not sure what's there for me."

«Don't you miss acting?»

"Yes and no. I miss the art. I miss the thrill. I don't miss Hollywood one bit. I don't miss the business or the culture. It's not like I've done any significant work for years. Besides, these past few days, I've felt like maybe I have a new role to play."

«Don't you need a job?»

Coop scratched at the stubble on his chin. "No. Not really. The money we made selling off the Box technology will pay all my outstanding debts and leave a lot left over. I don't have to give fifteen percent to Sylvia or pay taxes on it if I do it right. Huh. I bet Al knows a good accountant who could help with that."

«Sounds illegal to me.»

"Would that be a problem for you if it were?"

«Not especially, I'm just saying.»

"Good, because it's an American tradition to cheat on your taxes to whatever extent you can get away with."

«Huh. I did not know that.»

"Anyway…I already sent a transfer to cover my daughter's college expenses for the next few years. There's nothing else I can think of to throw cash at."

«But you could spend it. On stuff. That's a tradition too, isn't it?»

"Sure, and that's what I've always done. I chased money. I spent money. I acquired…stuff. In the end, I had nothing I cared about to show for it. Money doesn't buy happiness, Dyrk."

«I've watched a lot of movies, Ben. Nearly every one of them suggests otherwise.»

Coop laughed, which set Spud scampering over his neck to settle in on the opposite shoulder. "I guess they do, but they're wrong. Now that I have been able to take care of my kid and get rid of my debts, I realize that I'd do things differently. Getting this money didn't make me happy. It freed me from the prison of debt I'd created for myself. We have the chance to make a difference here, Dyrk. I can't remember the last time I could say that."

«I'll have to study this.»

"You do that. In the meantime, I'll come up with a plan for the Tots. We're now stuck with the little monsters. They're growing, and once they get their fur, they'll be even more insufferably cute." Coop rubbed the little alien's back, musing about potential courses of action.

A pair of identical teenagers entered the kitchen. Coop recognized Jess by her lab coat.

"Hey, Jess. Hey, Tycho."

"Good morning," offered Jess. Tycho gave him a nod.

Coop turned in his chair. Jess looked wide awake. Her hair was tied up, and she was already tapping on her tablet. In comparison, Tycho looked more like the zombie she had been. Each of them had a purple alien clinging to their shoulder. The original Potato was nowhere to be seen, probably sleeping like a lump back in the lab where they'd left it.

"Good morning. There's coffee on the counter. Also, Al called."

Tycho shuffled her way over to the coffee and poured herself a steaming mug before she joined Coop at the table. Jess remained standing but looked at Coop expectantly.

"What did Al have to say?"

"That we appear to be in the clear, for now."

"Your friends made it out?"

"Yep. The Box followed, all the way to Earth."

"Oh. They are persistent."

"Yeah. That's what I said. Did you have any revelations about these little guys overnight?"

Jess nodded her head. "Some. No answers, but I was able to stew over alien mitosis a bit."

"Say what?"

"Mitosis. The process by which a cell divides and creates two or more identical cells. It's the closest way to understand what is going on here."

Jess continued to talk, and Coop did his best to keep up despite her using terms like "prophase," "anaphase," and "metaphase."

He failed, and it showed.

Jess sighed. "You didn't understand any of that, did you?"

"Nope, but I think you are talking about the Tots, right?"

"Tots?"

"Yeah, Tater, Spud, and Junior. Yours is Junior, Tycho has Tater, and mine is Spud."

"You named them?"

«Duh! Why wouldn't he?»

"Sure. Why wouldn't I? How else are we going to tell them apart?"

"Mr. Cooper, biologically speaking, they're identical. There is no telling them apart."

Coop paused and looked from Jess to Tycho and back. "Isn't that true of you two, also?"

"I…" Jessica stammered before she fell silent.

«I want to try something. Back me up. Point to each of them and call it by name.»

Coop shrugged and pointed at Tycho's fuzzy golf ball that she was cradling in her hands. "That's Tater." He felt…something. Dyrk had done something. Incredibly, Tater perked up at the use of its name.

«Next one.»

"That's Junior." He pointed to Jess and on cue, her critter stuck its head out of her pocket and scrambled up her shirt to climb onto her head. "And this guy is Spud." Coop plucked Potato's offspring, or diploid, or whatever, from behind his ear, but at the use of its name (and another twinge that Dyrk was doing… something), it had jumped to his shoulder and scampered across his arm and back, then repeated the move on the other side.

"Fine, you've named them. Whatever. The point is, I think we should stay. They're yet another thing that needs to be studied, and there's no better lab anywhere on Earth than what I already have here."

"Except, we kind of promised it to Al," pointed out Cooper.

"Who's Al?" asked Tycho. "Do I know Al?"

"I told you about him," replied Coop. "He's an alien crime boss, but otherwise a helpful and delightful guy. I'll introduce you next time he drops by."

"Why would an alien crime boss just drop by?"

"For one thing, he owns this place and everything in it. He wants to sell all this science stuff that Jess is so attached to."

"Because I need it. Besides, he hasn't even secured a buyer yet. He'll get over it."

«Yeah, sure, because that's how crime bosses roll.»

"The point is, you still want to stay here on Titan."

"More than ever."

Coop shrugged. "And you can't do this work on Earth? I mean, we've got enough money to buy whatever you need, don't we?"

"We have money?" asked Tycho. "Do I have money too? And if so, how much?"

«Aww, our little girl is a mercenary. I guess that fits in with the whole war machine persona, right?»

Coop opted to ignore both Tycho and Dyrk for the moment.

"Maybe. If it were for sale." Jess sighed, a weary and depressed sound. "A lot of it is Box-design, unlike anything anywhere. Though, it's not just the equipment. It's...no one back on Earth is going to take me seriously."

"C'mon, you can't believe that. Your treatment of Potato's virus is responsible for curing three terminal people. You're going to be celebrated."

"No, I won't."

"Why the hell not?"

In answer, Jess pointed to Tycho and then to herself.

"What? I don't get it."

"I look like a pretty teenage girl, Mr. Cooper. I've been grappling with ageism and sexism my whole career, and I've just taken a huge step backward. The research community is going to take one look at me, and any credibility my past accomplishments had earned will go right out the window. I'll never get the chance to continue my own work. Others will push me aside and take it over."

«Unless she stays here.»

"Unless you stay here. Unless we stay here. Okay, so I guess that's settled."

Jessica's frustration melted away. "Really? You...you'll stay?"

Tycho shrugged. "My schedule's wide open, and I don't have anywhere to go. I mean, you told me everyone I knew is gone. If I stay, maybe you'll be able to recover some of my memories."

Jess patted Tycho's hand. "I will. I mean, I'll try. I promise."

"Dyrk and I talked it over earlier," responded Coop. "There are some things we want to explore, and you know, get to know one another better, outside of the crisis mode we've had since all this began. So, yeah, we'll stay, for a while."

The next morning, Dyrk prepared and served breakfast for everyone. They ate at the large table in the middle of the laboratory so Jess could hook Tycho to some machines. Coop ate a second serving, which was close to acknowledging that the viral echo was becoming a good cook. He didn't want to tell him for fear of it going to Dyrk's head. Which, of course, was Coop's head.

As he gathered the dishes, Coop walked behind Jess and cleared his throat. It was time to broach an uncomfortable topic.

He whispered, "You know the Box will come back, right?"

Jess set her tablet aside. "Yes. As long as we have Potato, they'll keep coming. Al bought us some time, but not enough. We need a solution."

«We need an arsenal.»

"Dyrk says we need more guns."

Tycho snorted, then paused, confused by Coop's nervous expression.

He glanced at the examination table where Tycho had been strapped down and where Potato had, more or less, given birth to three duplicates. The original, which had been so animated these last few days, hadn't moved an inch since producing the Tots. If anything, it was more of a lump than ever before. It was weird.

"Not to worry," he added. "Dyrk and I talked about that too, and we came up with a plan..."

CHAPTER THIRTY-ONE

Three days had passed since the trio had decided to stay on Titan. Jess was happy with the accommodations, but then she'd been living there for months prior to her experiments taking off. Being so focused on her work, she'd had no interest in anything approaching a creature comfort. Coop, on the other hand, was used to a certain amount of luxury—at a minimum, the aesthetic and ease of a well-equipped trailer. Tycho had no recollection of what she liked or wanted, and had remarked that as she'd been lying in a hospital bed since arriving on Titan, maybe a change to something a little nicer would be a good idea.

The solution, as suggested by Dyrk, was to call upon Al since the crime boss seemed to have his fingers into so many different pies. The xenon hadn't even blinked, which is how Coop wound up in the garage that morning, watching Al's associates unloading new furniture and supplies from a pair of large transports.

"We appreciate you letting us stay, and bringing all the supplies," Coop told him. "The Box weren't the best decorators."

Al favored him with a smile. "Happy to help. Besides, I've already made a fortune off your misfortune, and now, as an investor, I stand to make astronomical sums if Dr. Acorns develops any medical breakthroughs. It's a win-win scenario, as far as I'm concerned."

"It helps a lot. I just hope we can make progress before the Box come back."

"Let me worry about them. You have inspired me, Cooper. I no longer fear the Box, and that is a gift beyond price. Many things now become possible, but for the time being, you should focus on helping everyone recover. Make sure Dr. Acorns keeps working."

"As if I could stop her."

"That's good. How is the young lady, Tycho, doing?"

"Oh man, that girl is like a sponge. She follows Jess around and learns anything and everything she can. Science. How to run the machines. You name it. Maybe it's because she's a blank slate in the cognitive department, or maybe she was already a genius. Who knows? Either way, she's doing well."

"Very good to hear. Now, if you will excuse me, I need to go, Cooper. I'll stop by to check on you and my investment soon." Coop glanced up and realized the work crew had finished unloading, carried the furniture and other boxes inside, and piled into their respective transports. Al walked to his vehicle, and Coop returned inside the habitat so the Clusteran and his associates could open the garage and depart.

He found Jess and Tycho in the main laboratory with Potato and the Tots. The doctor had them on the examination table, where she and Tycho had connected a series of leads to each of the now cantaloupe-sized aliens.

The Tots seemed to be doing their best to tie the leads in knots by running around in circles. Potato, however, lay sedate and dormant.

"Can't you give them a sedative?"

"No. I tried. It had zero effect. If they don't stop running around, I may give myself one."

"I think they're fun and fascinating," Tycho opined. "They grow so fast."

"But how do they grow? They don't eat anything."

Jess shook her head. She tried to hold two of the Tots still. "I don't know. It's one of the many fascinating mysteries about them. They are capable of physical growth without any source of outside energy or nutrition. It shouldn't be possible, but they do it."

"Do they have different temperaments?" asked Coop. "I mean, right now, does one seem to be the ringleader?"

"Even though you named them, I still can't tell them apart when they're all together," complained Jess. She looked at Tycho. "Can you?"

The girl shook her head. "Nope."

«I can. They seem to have a rotation. It's like they've been taking turns with each of you these last few days.»

"Dyrk says he can tell them apart and that they've been rotating amongst us."

Jess glanced up. "Really? That's worth considering."

«Why?»

"Why?"

"Because the Tots are identical down to the cellular level. I'd like to understand what Dyrk can sense that allows him to differentiate between them, but not right now. I need to finish this scan before I tear my hair out."

"Okay, we'll come back to that. What's wrong with Potato?"

"I don't know, and it bugs me. Ever since it produced the Tots, it's been lethargic. Worse, its vitals are low, like it's shutting down. I did an electroencephalogram on Potato, and it shows little activity."

"What does the little guy have to think about?"

Jess shrugged. "That's just it. When I compare it to the data that Caja had compiled—"

"Who's Caja?" asked Tycho.

"One of the Box that had another research habitat here at the ranch."

"Caja was a jerk, but not as much of a douche as Pudełko."

"Okay, then who's Pudełko?"

"The other Box researcher in the other habitat. Except both of those habs are rubble now. You can see them if you look out the port of the far airlock."

"Yeah, because jerk and douche imploded their buildings before running home like babies."

«Well said, Ben.»

Jess rolled her eyes. "As I was saying, Caja's data showed a history of this same kind of minimal EEG readings. Potato's brain activity increased when I began showing it films. Now, everything seems to have been dialed back more than a year, to before I arrived here and began my work."

"Why not put Potato back in the film alcove in the playroom and let him soak up a couple hundred movies again?"

"I might, but not before I've finished my tests. I'm still trying to get EEGs of the Tots for comparison. They've got a lot more going on, and none of them have had any stimuli but us. If they'd just sit still long enough for me to hook them up…"

«Why doesn't she just ask Tycho to hold onto two of them at a time?»

Coop scratched his head. Thoughts of discretion and valor bounced through his mind. It was something he'd have to explain to Dyrk. Later.

"I'll get out of your way. But…when you have a minute, I want to run an idea by you."

"About what?"

"About how to get the Box to leave us alone. Permanently."

Dinner had been incredible. Dyrk had dug through some of the supplies Al had provided and created something that looked like a bland protein loaf in a lump of carb paste but tasted like Beef Wellington and Yukon Gold mashed potatoes. Everyone had seconds. Conversational topics had included Tycho's plans for decorating her room and some of the common areas, lovingly detailed without pause while she shoveled dinner into her food hole and chewed around her words. Jess reported that as best she could figure things, Potato had regressed to a state identical to a year ago and for the previous century—an immortal lump. Coop and Jess explained to Tycho about Dyrk, what he was and how he'd come to be. Throughout the explanation, Tycho's mouth hung open. It was the only time she'd stopped eating.

After dinner, while Tycho volunteered to do the dishes, Coop took Jess to the communications center.

"What are we doing here?" Jess asked.

"I told you Dyrk and I came up with a plan, right?"

"Yes."

"Do you trust me?"

"I trust you, but I find your judgment to be suspect."

«She's not wrong.»

"That's fair, but we gave this some thought. Now I just need you to contact the Box."

Jessica's eyebrows shot up. "Isn't that what we're trying to avoid?"

"Not exactly. We're trying to avoid the Box killing us. If my plan works—and it will," he added quickly, "We'll be able to get them off our backs. Forever."

Jess crossed her arms. "What's this plan?"

«She looks a little skeptical. Is that normal?»

In my experience, women are often skeptical of men making big promises. To be fair, it is justified.

Coop laid out his plan. Jess asked some good questions, but in the end, she relented.

The doctor sat at the communications terminal. "Who should I send it to?"

"Is there a directory?"

"I'll check." Jess poked around the computer. "Yep, but it isn't very large. Let's see...yeah. This might work. There is a Box named 'Apoti,' and her title is—"

"Her?"

Jess gave Coop a cold look. "All Box names are inflected for one of five genders. Most are gender neutral, though that can change if they alter their avatars. Apoti is marked as feminine. Now, as I was saying, her title is 'Research Director.' Based on what I know of the Box, that would be an important position."

"Okay. That sounds like our best bet."

Jess typed out her message.

From: Scatola
To: Apoti

Hello. My name is Theca. I live on Titan and some lady handed me a fuzzy little animal and told me to contact you. She said its name is Potato. It's totally cute. She said I could ask you for a reward if you wanted it back. Her letter said to come here and message you from this account. I guess I'll hang out for a bit. You know, this place is kinda nice. So, message me back.

Jess finished typing and sat back in her chair. "Your message makes me sound like an idiot."

"That is part of the plan."

"Okay. It could take hours or days for them to respond. Meanwhile, I have work to do." Jess stood and made it halfway to the door before the comms suite beeped, announcing the arrival of an incoming message.

From: Apoti
To: Scatola

Dear Theca, Thank you for contacting me. You are correct. Potato belongs to us, and we would be willing to offer a reward for its safe return. Please let me know what you desire as compensation for keeping it safe and returning it. I can arrive on Titan in two days. I await your urgent reply.

"Well, well," Jess muttered. "It worked."

Coop shrugged. "Phase one worked. We still have to pull off the transfer."

"Right. What should I say?"

"That's the easy part. Tell her we want the Box ranch, free and clear, and all the equipment in it. Tell her if she signs it over, we'll be happy to return Potato to her when she arrives."

CHAPTER THIRTY-TWO

Two days later—after another incredible dinner and one culinary disaster that Dyrk was still apologizing for—Apoti arrived at the ranch in a sleek ATV unlike anything on Titan. As Coop waited for the atmosphere to change out, he gazed at the vehicle with the admiration men have shown for well-crafted transportation since the days when the first Romans detailed their chariots with gold filigrees of flames. He wondered if the Box had brought it with her.

Coop stepped into the garage and waited for Apoti to exit the vehicle. He and Dyrk had spent the previous two days working on his disguise for this moment. Dyrk hadn't begrudged the time. They'd agreed he needed to learn how to finesse Coop's DNA. It had hurt like hell at first, but Dyrk soon got the hang of it, and the results were incredible.

Now he stood in the garage looking like a five-foot-five-inch man of East Asian heritage, with a lethargic blue-green striped alien tucked under his left arm.

"Dyrk, I just want to say again that this is the best makeup job I've ever had."

«Thanks, Coop. Now you need to give the performance of a lifetime.

Because if you don't, we'll all be killed at some point in the not-too-distant future.»

"Thanks for the reminder."

«My pleasure.»

Coop sighed.

The door of the Box vehicle lifted, and Apoti stepped out.

«That's new. Wow.»

"Mmm, hmm."

Apoti was different. Apoti was—in Coop's estimation—smoking hot. If one found mechanical avatars attractive. Which he was almost certain he did not. Almost.

The Box stood six feet tall and had a slender build. Her faux flesh was supple and held a pigment that reminded Coop of fresh-cut cedar. It was exotic and alluring.

Apoti was also well-attired and stunning. She wore a pair of slim-cut seersucker pants that flared at the bottom over stylish flats with a sapphire finish. Her top was a sleeveless diaphanous affair of purest white. It did nothing to disguise the avatar's well-designed...enhancements.

"Those seem wholly unnecessary."

«Are you complaining?»

"No, but I'm thinking we would have been better off letting Jess handle this transaction."

«I can take over if you need me to.»

Coop stopped himself from laughing out loud.

"You're the only person worse than me for this job. I mean, who in their right mind would trust an action hero with anything, with cleavage like that around? You'd sell us out in a heartbeat."

Dyrk offered no reply.

Apoti glided across the garage and extended a manicured bio-mechanical hand.

"You must be Theca. I am Apoti."

Coop shook her hand. It was soft. He forced himself to look up and meet her eyes.

«Is that shade of blue even legal? She should need a license to wield those things.»

You are not wrong.

"Nice to meet you, Apoti. Is this your pet?"

Apoti's face twitched. It was the first time she looked artificial.

"Potato is much more than a pet, but yes, it's mine. I am grateful to you for recovering it. Could you perhaps tell me more about how it happened? I just want to understand fully."

«You're on.»

Coop stroked Potato's back and put on a mien of casual stupidity.

"Oh, this little dude. Yeah, I was hanging out at the spaceport a few days ago. Sometimes I can get work hauling luggage and stuff, you know. So, I was sitting down, and this lady comes walking in with an older dude and her little sister or something. She was pushing that chick on a hover bed. I thought she looked kinda dead, but kinda cute too."

Apoti maintained a smile but motioned for Coop to move things along.

"Where was I? Oh yeah, so she walks up to me and I think, this chick is into me. She probably was. I've lost some weight, you know? And I've been working out. She says she's in a hurry to leave and asks if I'd like to set myself up. So I said, sure. I wasn't busy that day. Then she hands me this little dude and an envelope. I thought the envelope would have cash, but it just had a letter with instructions on how to contact you. The letter said you'd make me rich."

Apoti nodded. "I understand, and I appreciate you taking the time to tell me. Now, you said you would like the deed to the property comprising this ranch, as well as this habitat and all property contained therein, is that correct?"

"Yep. I wanna get into biotech."

"Truly? Do you have expertise in this arena?"

Coop shrugged his shoulders. "Not really, but how hard can it be?"

Apoti smiled again. "Of course. I wish you luck. Now, if I might have Potato?"

"Oh, sure." Coop handed the little alien over with a fond pat on its head.

Potato didn't react at all. Coop sighed on the inside. He'd miss Potato. They'd been through a lot, but he also knew Potato didn't remember any of it. The way Jess had explained it, giving birth to the Tots—the alien mitosis whatsis—had reset the little guy to its original biological settings. She'd felt confident about that. She'd been less sure whether it had been a natural part of its biology or something the virus had triggered.

Apoti took Potato in one hand and began to lift her shirt with the other.

«Oh, my.»

Coop looked at the ceiling.

Apoti stared at him and opened a panel, revealing a cavity in her torso. She put Potato inside and closed it back. Then she produced a tablet.

"This contains the deed and a letter authorizing its transfer to your corporation. I trust you will find everything is in order."

Coop accepted the tablet. Everything checked out. "So, it's all mine?"

"You are welcome to it, Mr. Theca. I suspect it will be a long time before any Box return to this moon, perhaps even the entire solar system. It has not been a good experience for us. Those that had insisted upon it are now...out of favor."

"Thank you, Apoti."

"It was my pleasure. Do we have any business left to attend to?"

Coop almost said 'no.' Almost. "We could get dinner to celebrate. I could show you around Titan."

Apoti's face didn't move one single bit. She simply turned on a fancy heel and returned to her dream vehicle.

Coop watched her walk away.

Dyrk sighed in his head.

«You can't blame a guy for trying.»

CHAPTER THIRTY-THREE

Three Weeks Later

Coop set his tablet aside and looked around the new and improved common room. Tycho had shown a real flair for decorating, though he still felt a touch of annoyance at having been outvoted about a classic pinball machine by the wet bar.

But it wasn't just the common room. The entire habitat had evolved for the better. Much better. It still held copious amounts of laboratory equipment—in fact, more had arrived. It also had real furniture now, much of it in bright-colored fabrics, black leather, and chrome.

«Ben, is there a term for this style of decorating?»

The actor considered. "Yeah, it's called 'tech-startup.' I could live without the beanbag chairs, but the rest of the stuff is nice enough."

Jess and Tycho walked into the room. Coop could tell them apart because Jess owned the only lab coat in the place and always wore it. A fact that helped him more often than he liked to admit.

"Hello, ladies. I just had a message from Al."

The identical women stopped and looked at him expectantly. "What did he have to say?" Jess asked.

"He said that when Doos got to Earth, it got itself in a bit of a pickle. Apparently, its extensions accosted some innocent civilians. Now there's a lawsuit, and the Box are trying to settle things quietly."

"Was anyone hurt?" asked Tycho.

"No. It didn't sound like it. In fact, it sounds like things will work out just fine for Lilly and her siblings."

Jessica nodded. "That's good news. Let's hope Doos will leave everyone alone now."

"Amen to that. Are you ladies up for some dinner?"

Jess and Tycho readily agreed. The group retired to their new dining room in what used to be Potato's playpen of sensory stimuli. Tycho had removed most of the toys, starting with the ones that made noise or emitted odors. She had also painted the walls a soothing ecru and installed a modest lighting fixture, an elegant banquet table, and plenty of chairs so they could have guests should they ever opt to host dinner parties. Until such a time, it was just the three of them, and they clustered together at one end of the table. The Tots played on the psychedelic floor with colors pulsing while they rollicked from one spot to another, and the humans tucked into their meal.

Coop and Dyrk had worked out a timetable so the viral echo could continue his culinary practice every night, and he hadn't had a repeat of the ghost pepper disaster. In fact, the last several dinners had been so good that conversation had been suspended until dessert so they could all savor the food on their plates. Dyrk had been so chuffed, he'd gone all out tonight, and the dessert course had been a flaming Baked Alaska that astounded Tots and humans alike.

Coop pushed his plate back and licked the last bits of ice cream from his lips. "So, Jess, I don't want to pressure you, but how is the research coming along?"

Dr. Acorns set her fork down, her eyes coming back into focus as if realizing she'd finished the dessert on her plate and there wasn't any more. Dyrk had found her weak spot: sweets.

"Really well. It isn't ready for primetime yet, but everything is moving along even better than expected."

"That's great news."

"It is miraculous news, Mr. Cooper. If things continue like this, we may be able to offer cures for almost all ills. In fact, the effects would be so sweeping that it would require some serious debate."

"What do you mean?"

"For better or worse, diseases help manage population. We've already overpopulated one planet, and we're spreading into the galaxy like locusts. What happens when people stop dying prematurely?"

Coop tried to wrap his head around the consequences. It hurt. "I see your point, but does that mean you should stop?"

Jess shook her head. "No. Absolutely not. We don't retard science, but it will require a robust debate."

"And you think Earth's leaders will be up to that?" asked Tycho.

Coop and Jess both stayed silent. The doctor opted to change the subject.

"So, Mr. Cooper, have you given any thought to what you'd like to do now?"

"I have a few ideas. Do you think the people here on Titan might welcome community theater?"

"I doubt it," replied Jess. "I've never seen any indication of art or creativity here."

"Is community theater what I think it is?" asked Tycho.

"Amateur stage productions. Well beneath me, but…you know, it would give me something to do."

"If it keeps you out of my hair, I'm all for it."

"Could I do it too?" asked Tycho.

Coop gave Tycho an appraising look.

«She'd be great at learning lines. Besides, I can make her look like anyone.»

Coop checked his inventory of smiles and found that the one he wanted matched the genuine expression on his face: a beaming grin of encouragement. "Honey, I think you'd be a natural actress."

"Oh no, I don't want to be on stage. It would be weird to act like I was someone else when I'm still trying to remember who I was before the coma."

«She makes a fine point.»

"Then what?"

"Well, what I really want to do is direct."

The End

AUTHORS' NOTE: REACHING THE END

Well, you've done it, reached the end of the *Adrenaline Rush*, our science fiction trilogy. If we're being totally honest, we had far too much fun writing these books. Truly, it was a nice turn of events to tell a tale about a virus that actually saved lives. But s satisfying as that was, it was also just part of a larger theme that we like to pursue not just in the fiction we write, but what we read as well. It goes by many names. Satisfaction. Closure. Completion. It's all about how when you reach the end of a story, the various loose ends are accounted for and everything gets tied up with a neat bow by the end of the *denouement*. Ideally, the good guys have won and the bad guys have been vanquished—and maybe even redeemed. Yes, unavoidably, sacrifices had been made, but we're left with a clear sense that they were necessary and the resulting outcomes worth the price that was paid.

We want our stories, our real like life stories, to end that way, to resolve with positive outcomes, with things that make sense, sometimes even with a warm fuzzy feeling so that it's easier for us to get up the next morning and face the challenges of the new day. We know it probably won't be effortless. We know we will face trials and tribulations, but like the characters in the books we love, we too have a story arc. We'd like to think that we'll grow, develop, and improve over the course of our respective arcs.

Coop is a good example. We had a lot of feedback about him from the earliest days of Book One. We can admit it now, he wasn't very likable. A few readers asked why we expected them to spend their time reading about a character like that, and we said "Wait. Just wait. Yes he's near the end of his life. Yes, he's seriously flawed. But if you'll just give him a chance—as the story itself gives him a second chance—he'll get his act together. With a little help he'll grow into a much more likable human being, an asset to those around him and a friend those in need."

Taken as a whole the *Adrenaline Rush* trilogy can be seen as a story of redemption. It's all there in the subtext. We're not saying you should go looking for the subtext, it's okay to let it sneak up on you long after you've finished the book. If all you found as you read this trilogy was a cool story about a washed-up drunk who's given a second chance at life courtesy of the newborn, alien intelligence in his head, bar fights against outrageous odds, biologically based science fiction tropes that revolved around an awesomely cute alien critter, multiple sequences illustrating the classic battle of man versus machine with lots of smashing and blasting and a few near misses that could have ended everything, well, that's fine too.

We'd like to think we've tied everything off with a neat bow, but we also know we left plenty of loose ends and open questions, just in case we ever wanted to come back and tell the next story. Now that our heroes are safe on Titan, what does the future hold in store for them? Will Tycho regain her memories? Will Jess rise above her somewhat questionable ethical choices and utilize her discoveries to save people from illness and disease. Will Coop make good on his realization that his life can be used for more than just satisfying his ego? Will Dyrk go on to become a master chef? What about Al, one of the few survivors of his race, once a gifted performer and now a powerful crime boss who has learned that the impossible is possible? What lies ahead for Big Tony and the Diamond Queen? What will happen with the tots—Tater, Spud, and Junior—and will they remain interchangeable fuzzballs or will they each develop their own quirks, idiosyncrasies, and abilities? And what about the Box, are they gone for good or will they return with even more nefarious extensions?

So, yeah, there's no shortage of loose threads which we could tug on to pursue additional storylines. Whether we do or not is somewhat up to *you*. We're content to let things lie with how this book ends. We provided a good amount of closure and a satisfying ending, but if you don't agree, if you want more, if you want to see Jess do her part to end human suffering, if you want to see if Coop is really as the brilliant actor as he thinks he is, and if you'd like to find out if Tycho has the chops to be half as good a director as she is a mindless war machine, then let us know. Leave a review for this book—and/or either of the other two in the trilogy—and tell us what you'd like to see. It could be something as simple as saying "I want *more!*" and if enough of you do that, well, we'll have no choice but to listen and give you what you're asking for

Lawrence M Schoen
Bryan Thorne
September 2022

ACKNOWLEDGMENTS

Anger Management was originally produced under a wee bit of duress. Lawrence spent weeks in the hospital for cancer treatment during its production and endured the suffering of recovery for months to follow. It wasn't easy and it often made work next to impossible, but thanks to the efforts of his medical team and caregivers, especially Valerie, he made it through and this book is now in your hands. In particular, he would like to acknowledge the work, prayers, and kind wishes of his family, friends, and fans who helped maintain his spirits through an incredibly trying time.

We would also like to thank our initial beta-readers. Dr. James Caplan and Karin O'Callaghan. They were great! When this book moved to LMBPN, we had a whole new set of incredible beta-readers that we'd like to thank. Huge thanks to Rachel Beckford, Larry Omans, Kelly O'Donnell, John Ashmore, and Mary Morris. We'd also like to thank our new editor, Jacqui Scherrer. Each of these people do astonishing work making us look like we know what we're doing. We are our beyond grateful to them. Along similar lines, LMBPN also hooked us up with Jake Clark. He turned in the gorgeous cover art for this book (as well as its predecessors), and he is clearly our go-to-guy for illustrating mindless teenage war machines. Thanks, Jake!

As always, we want to acknowledge our readers. Without you, writing this book would lose all meaning. You give us purpose and fuel our passion.

Finally, as we try to remember to do with every book (because we don't want to get locked out of our respective houses), we gratefully acknowledge and thank the women in our lives who put up with the all too often incomprehensible behavior of a pair of authors. We are not worthy and we know it. They know we know it. And we know they know we know it.

ABOUT BRIAN THORNE

Brian Thorne is a former Marine and intelligence officer. These days, he works in cybersecurity when he's not playing chauffeur to his son or training his new rescue dog. If those activities allow him spare time, he tries to write.

A recent transplant to Texas, Thorne has undertaken a noble quest to find the perfect brisket and share news of it with the world. He views it as his crowning contribution to humanity.

To follow Brian on his writing adventure, keep up to date on his brisket quest, and receive a free short story, you can join his newsletter at http://bit.ly/ThorneNews. Your email address will not be sold, rented, or in any other way disseminated.

ABOUT LAWRENCE M. SCHOEN

Lawrence M. Schoen holds a Ph.D. in cognitive psychology and psycholinguistics. He spent ten years as a college professor, doing research in the areas of human memory and language. This was followed by seventeen years as the director of research for a medical center in Philadelphia that provided mental health and addiction services.

He's also the founder of the Klingon Language Institute, and since 1992, he has championed the exploration and use of this constructed tongue throughout the world. In addition, he occasionally works as a hypnotherapist specializing in authors' issues. He is also a cancer survivor.

In 2007, he was a finalist for the Astounding Award for Best New Writer. He received a Hugo Award nomination for Best Short Story in 2010 and Nebula Award nominations for Best Novella in 2013, 2014, 2015, and 2018, for Best Novelette in 2019, and for Best Novel in 2016.

Some of his most popular writing deals with the ongoing humorous adventures of a spacefaring stage hypnotist named the Amazing Conroy and his companion animal Reggie, an alien buffalito that can eat anything and farts oxygen.

His *Barsk* series represents his serious work and uses anthropomorphic SF to explore ideas of prophecy, intolerance, political betrayal, speaking to the dead, predestination, and free will. It's also earned him the Cóyotl Award for Best Novel of 2015 and again in 2018.

Lawrence lives near Philadelphia with his wife Valerie, who is neither a psychologist nor a Klingon speaker.

If you would like updates on Lawrence's new releases, appearances, or special offers, please consider joining his mailing list. Your email address will not be sold, rented, or in any other way disseminated. Simply use this link to sign up: http://bit.ly/LMS-join

ALSO BY LAWRENCE M. SCHOEN

Barsk

Barsk: The Elephants' Graveyard

(2015 Nebula Award Finalist, 2015 Winner Cóyotl Award)

The Moons of Barsk

(2018 Winner Cóyotl Award)

Excerpts of Jorl ben Tral

Soup of the Moment

Pizlo's Limits

SERIES IN THE "CONROYVERSE"

Conroyverse: A Sampler

("Buffalo Dogs," *Buffalito Destiny, Ace of Corpses*, and *Slice of Entropy*)

The Amazing Conroy

Buffalito Bundle

(includes "Yesterday's Taste," 2011 WSFA Small Press Award Finalist)

Barry's Tale

(2012 Nebula Award Finalist)

Calendrical Regression

(2014 Nebula Award Finalist)

Barry's Deal

(2017 Nebula Award Finalist)

Buffalito Destiny

Trial of the Century

(2013 Nebula Award Finalist)

Buffalito Contingency

Command Performance

(The Amazing Conroy Omnibus Edition)

Freelance Courier

Ace of Corpses

Ace of Saints

Ace of Thralls

Ace of Agency

(Freelance Courier Books 1 – 3)

Pizza In Space

Slice of Entropy

Slice of Chaos

Humaniversity (with Catherine M. Petrini)

Dorms of Asgard

Pirates of Sol

Pirates of Marz

Seeds of War (with Jonathan Brazee)

Invasion

Scorched Earth

Bitter Harvest

Seeds of War Trilogy

Adrenaline Rush (with Brian Thorne)

Fight or Flight

Alien Thrill Seeker

Anger Management

The Demon Codex (with Brian Thorne)

Soul Bottles

At the Speed of Yeti

Undead Alternatives

Collections

Creature Academy:

Cautionary Poems of Public Education

Sweet Potato Pie and other stories

The Rule of Three and other stories

Openings without Closure

Transcendent Boston and other stories

Non-Fiction

Eating Authors: One Hundred Writers'

Most Memorable Meals

Author Website:

http://www.lawrencemschoen.com/books/

OTHER BOOKS FROM LMBPN PUBLISHING

Sign up for the LMBPN email list to be notified of new releases and special deals!

https://lmbpn.com/email/

For a complete list of books by LMBPN please visit:

https://lmbpn.com/books-by-lmbpn-publishing/

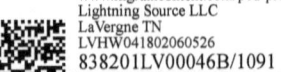

www.ingramcontent.com/pod-product-compliance
Lightning Source LLC
LaVergne TN
LVHW041802060526
838201LV00046B/1091
* 9 7 9 8 8 8 5 4 1 8 4 8 5 *